KINSEY

PENNINGTON FAMILY Book 1

KATHI S. BARTON

World Castle Publishing, LLC
Pensacola, Florida
Copyright © 2025 Kathi S. Barton
Hardback ISBN: 9798292550341
Paperback ISBN: 9798891264465
eBook ISBN: 9798891264472
First Edition World Castle Publishing, LLC, July 21, 2025
http://www.worldcastlepublishing.com
Licensing Notes
Cover: Cover Designs by Karen
Editor: Karen Fuller

Chapter 1

Kinsey didn't want to go to the bank to get a loan. Getting a loan for a new hot water tank seemed to be fruitless to him, especially since he knew that he'd get turned down and have to go all summer without hot water to take a shower. It really sucked being broke all the time. Wylie came into the house when he was getting his tie tied.

"Going to the bank?" He told him about the hot water tank. "It's too bad that we can't make arrangements to pay in the fall. That's when the crops are in and we can afford things like this."

"Barely. Just when I think we can put a little by for a few months, something like this happens." Kinsey asked if he wanted to go with him. "I mean, we can get a sandwich at the dairy bar. I've got just about enough for that."

"Nah, I have to go into town anyway, but at the other end. Mr. Thomson said he had some work for me to do. Not that I can spare the time, but I know a little cash right now would go a long way. Have you thought about taking him up on his offer of plowing his fields and then ours? It sure would be nice to have a better tractor to get the fields up and going this year. We could even do that extra fifty acres that we couldn't last year."

"I already told him that I'd do it. And if I help him with the planting, he'll let me use his tractor for planting and harvesting as well. Those fifty acres would be a good deal easier to plant with his tractor." They made plans to meet up in town at about two. That way, they could get the other supplies that were needed to plant the rest of the fields once they got the tractors going. "I thought that we could use ours, too, even though it's old. Having two tractors going at once would get twice the work done in half the time. I mean, so long as old Tim — who named the tractor that anyway? At least until he poops out on us again."

It took him a while to get his truck going. It had been his granddas vehicle when he'd been alive, and he'd been babying it along since he'd passed away. Like a lot of things on the farm, they needed to get a replacement for that as well. But things never seemed to come to fruition for them in the fall. He thought again about giving up the farm and getting a steady job that had insurance with it.

The banker was out to lunch when he finally got to the bank. It was just barely eleven o'clock when he got there, and he'd be out until one. He wondered if he could have a job like that one. Where you could justify a two-hour lunch. Sitting on one of the benches that he'd been wearing a soft spot in for years, he thought about having another job. The others did.

Wylie helped him around the farm. They had two hundred head of cattle that needed to be milked daily. Then they sold the milk to the Amish so that they could make their cheese. It was the only really good-paying part of the farm. They also sold off some of the cattle for meat. It was their only source of dairy and meat they had on the farm, if you didn't count the occasional fish or two they'd get from the pond.

Gleason had an outside job. He worked for one of the local farms doing what he did by himself. Planting and harvesting the fruits of their labor was something that kept them afloat through the winter months when no other money was coming in. He'd even do that if there were a place that paid well enough.

The other three had different jobs that took them all over the state. Raphael drove a semi for a large company. While it paid well, Raphael, his brother, wasn't around as much as they'd like. He would usually be home late on Saturday afternoon and have to go out again late Sunday evening. When he was able to get home, that was.

His younger brothers Bodi and Ara worked in town. Bodi at the gas station which again paid well but work was sparce. Ara worked for the newspaper as a reporter and seemed to love his job a great deal.

They all worked the farm when they had time off, but he and Wiley worked from sunup to sundown and sometimes well into the next day. The spring and fall were their busiest times of the year. Not that they didn't work in the other two seasons, but it was just longer hours in those two seasons.

"What's your name?" He had not heard the kid come up to him and smiled at her. After telling her his first name, she smiled. "My name is Kelley. My dad said I'm not supposed to talk to strangers, but if I tell you my first name and you tell me yours, we're not strangers anymore, are we?"

"I guess not, but I don't think that you telling people your name is what he meant." She got up on the seat next to him and took his hand into her tiny one. "Where is your daddy, honey? I don't think he meant for you to come sit by me."

"He's talking to the woman at the counter. He likes her and thinks she'll make a good momma for me. I don't know. She seems to have a lot of playdough on her face, don't you think?" He couldn't help it; he burst out laughing. Everyone turned to look at him, but her daddy and the woman with a playdough face. "I don't care if I have a momma anyway. The one I had just up and left me one night when her and daddy were fighting."

Alarm bells went off in his head, but he didn't so much as blink at the little girl. Talking to her about her momma seemed to be all she wanted to talk about, so he just nodded and kept his mouth shut. While talking to the little girl, he looked around for someone who could entertain her besides himself. When the banker came into the bank, Kinsey decided that he needed to get away from the little girl, or he was going to be embroiled in some kind of murder investigation and didn't want that at all.

Standing up, he told her that he had to go and left her on the bench. As soon as he was in the banker's office, he let out a long breath that had him slightly dizzy. The banker, Mr. Howard, asked him if he was all right.

"I don't know." Shivering, he just told him what was going on and how much he didn't want to be involved in a murder arrest. Howard got up from his desk and looked at the man at the counter when he pointed him out. "Do you know him or his wife?"

"No. I've never seen them before. When he leaves, I'll talk to Candance and see what he had to say." He sat back down at his desk. "I guess you're in here for a loan to tide you over until fall. I can't do that, son. I wish that I could. But you don't have enough income on your own to get much more than five hundred dollars."

"I'll take that." Looking a little shocked, he told him about the hot water heater. And while he could afford small payments of about a hundred a month, he couldn't outright pay for it. "I wouldn't need it for a year, just about six months should do it."

"You'd need to take it out for at least two years. If you pay it off early, that's up to you. Kinsey, what if I could loan you five thousand dollars? I could make that sneak by the board, I think. If not, then we've already done it. Would that help you? The payments wouldn't be much over a hundred dollars for five years." Boy, was it tempting, but did he need five grand? "You could not just get yourself a hot water heater, but you could put some real money into that truck of yours to keep it running. Or even buy you something newer. I think that truck is about as old as you are."

"It's actually older." He thought about what he'd do with the money and decided that if he was going to get the loan, he was going to pay off his bill at the feed store, too. As well as be able to get some real groceries in the house that would last a while. "I'll take it. Tell me what the payments will be, and I'll tell you if I can get that much. Thanks, Mr. Howard. I thought for sure you were going to turn me down."

"You never told me that you were in the service, Kinsey. I wish you had, I would have tried a bit harder to get you some money all those times you came in here." He said that he'd been out for three years. "Doesn't matter. You did this town proud by keeping us safe, and I want to be one who can help you out."

The payments were something that he could manage. It would be tight, but he'd have a hot water heater as well as his feed bill paid off for the cattle. Getting the check, he went out and cashed it to do what needed to be done. As soon as he was finished, Mr. Howard brought him back to his office.

"She left him, he said. The man at the counter. Told Candance that she had up and left him in the middle of the night. I'm going to have Rosie look into things. She's a good cop and does all right for this town. She'll know how to ask the right questions. Sure did make me nervous when you came in here. I'll let you know what they find out." He thanked him and noticed that the little girl was gone as well. After telling him her name, he left the bank.

Heading to the hardware store, he ordered a hot water heater for the house. He got the size that should have been in the house and thought it would be wonderful to have enough hot water to take a shower long enough to wash his hair and his body. Laughing to himself, he was proud of the way he was getting things done and was happy that Mr. Howard had thought so well of him. Then he went to the feed store.

The bill wasn't as large as he'd thought it should have been, so he had a bit more left over than he thought. Going to the grocery store with enough money to buy all the things that he needed, he was thrilled beyond words that it took him three trips to take it all into the house. The hot water heater would be in tomorrow, and he'd have to install it, but he was actually looking forward to it. Something that he usually dreaded, he was going to map out the entire morning for getting it done. The others would be thrilled to know that they'd be able to take a long shower too.

It was nearly three o'clock when Wylie came back from his meeting. Telling him about the bank loan and how he'd been able to use the money, he got a bear hug from his younger brother. As soon as they sat down to dinner that night, not only had Gleason made it home for dinner, but so did Bodi and Ara. It was a good night to have fresh vegetables at the table with their beef steaks.

All of them had a hand in cooking when they were home. Usually, they had stuff that was easy to put on in the morning and eat in the evening. His favorite thing to make was chili, but it had been too hot to have over the past week, so they'd been eating a lot of steaks and pot roasts. Kinsey decided that if he ever got a job that paid well, he was never going to have another crock pot meal as long as he lived.

"I'm going to be working with Mr. Thomson in his fields for the next three weeks. I know that we still have to get our crops in, but he said that he'd let me go before dark, and I could use his tractor to put out things in too. Great deal and he's paying me five hundred a week to help him out." They all congratulated him on his job and the money. It would come in handy when they were making payments on the bank loan. He told them about the feed store and the groceries, as well as the hot water heater. "I'm looking forward to having enough water to take a shower to get myself clean. Not to mention using the washer for my clothing. It's hard to get them clean when the water is freezing cold."

Dinner was an easy clean-up with all five of them working at it. There was money left over, so he made sure that each of them got a bit of it. He'd had the most fun buying groceries for the first time this year, at least everything that they needed, so he didn't take a cut of the money. The others were to use their part for something they'd been wanting to do, and he smiled when Ara said he was going to use his to get himself some socks. They were a bunch of men who had been too long without a woman around, and that was all he could think about.

The heater arrived just as he was finishing up with the cattle. There had been some trouble with the milkers at first, but he'd been able to fix that without any trouble. As soon as things were set up with the heater, getting it installed in about half the time that he thought it would take, he jumped into the shower and cleaned up. It was wonderful to have enough water to get clean without freezing at the end of it.

Setting the washer to wash his things up, he headed back out to the barn. There was always something that needed fixing, and today was no different. As he finished up with the tractor, thinking that he could get at least another year or two out of it, Wylie came over with the neighbor's tractor and started plowing the land for it. But first, he plowed up the garden that he planted every year so that they'd have fresh produce when they wanted it. He was still putting the tomatoes in the ground when Mr. Howard came by to see him.

"I wanted to tell you that the police might come talk to you about what Kelley told you. It seems that the missus is missing, and Tom can't give a good excuse for where she might have gone. Kelley is in protective custody right now until her grandma can come and get her. They've arrested Tom, I guess, on suspicion of murder." That was a shocker. "I told them that he was hitting up on Candance when he was in the bank and that the kid talked to you. Good thing, I guess, or there would be no telling how long she might have gone missing without anyone knowing."

"She told me that her mom was fighting with her daddy." Mr. Howard told him that's what he'd told them. "I don't really want to get involved, but I will. I just hope she's someplace far away and will turn up someday. Little Kelley can't believe that she'd left her behind on her birthday."

Just as Howard was getting in his car to leave, a cruiser pulled into the long drive. He really didn't want to get involved in anything, but knew that if it was his sister, he'd want someone to tell him where she was. Telling the police he had three more tomatoes to plant, could they wait, he'd take them in the house. They were agreeable, especially if he had some tea brewed for a drink or two. He had some that he brewed just that morning and invited them into the house.

~*~

"I don't understand why they have put her into the system instead of waiting for someone to go and get her. It's right here in the paper that she is put in the system." Grannie said she didn't know, but the little girl was going to have to live with someone. "I'll drive Ms. Stacker if it comes to that. You don't want to have a five-year-old cooped up on a bus for an hour while getting to your house. It'll drive both of them crazy."

Meggie knew that she'd have to call the meeting she was having in the morning off, but it was better than her worrying about Ms. Stacker and her granddaughter traveling on a bus as well as having to tote that little grandson of hers too as well. Ms. Stacker had lost her ability to drive about a year ago, and she'd been taking her all over town when she needed it. Instead, she'd hint around that she had a doctor's appointment, and Meggie would end up taking her and the little boy. Her grannie was the same way about driving.

Not that she minded. She loved her grannie and was so happy that grannie had decided to live with her full-time. It was great for them both. Meggie would come home to a nice meal, and Grannie could watch her shows all day without being disturbed. The nursing home that she was in would plan activities for those few hours, and Grannie would have to miss them. The activities, not her shows.

"I hate that you have to miss work." She wanted to tell her grannie that she did as well, but didn't. Her grannie was all she had, and she was never going to miss an opportunity to be with her over a meeting or something equally boring. "I was thinking that next week, when I have those tests done, I'll use that driver you talked about."

"You don't have to do that. I don't mind being there when you have your tests. I know you hated having someone drive you around, too." She said that sometimes it was necessary. "Yes, and I'll let you know when I can't cancel something, and you'll use him. For now, the two of us are working things out. Besides, you give me the best advice when I'm working. Did you know that Landry Lending is closing up? I heard about it yesterday. I wonder why he didn't come to me about a loan."

"He's too prideful, that man is. And you being a woman would have just set him on his ears. Stupid man. He'd rather close up his only business rather than come to you about money troubles. I heard it was his wife who was making him close the doors. That'll put fifteen people out of work, and it being summer and all." She asked what summer had to do with that. "Child care. They won't have their kids in school to go job hunting, and they can't afford a sitter anymore. Just a terrible shame it is that people don't think about the ones they're affecting when they do something like close their doors after fifty some years."

"I never thought about school being out either. Do you think I should go talk to him or let him close up? I can hire his people, some of them anyway, but I don't know about seeing him." She said that those people would need a good job if they were going to make it until Christmas. "I'll talk to Landry and see if you can get a list of his employees that he's putting out of work. Maybe I can talk to him about shutting his doors, too."

"Don't bother. Mrs. Landry has a list of things

that she wants to do with her husband now that he has time for them. She wants to go on a cruise like the two of us did last year. Remember how much fun we had? Oh, to be able to live like that daily." She told her that if she wanted, she could take a cruise for the summer. "No, it wouldn't be as fun without you there. You liven things up when we're together."

They had had fun. A great deal of it seeing the Bahamas like they had. And spending a week on a large ship had been the best trip she'd had in some time. Her cell phone would have worked had she brought it with her, but she'd left it at home, so she couldn't be bothered. Yes, she thought again, it was the best trip ever.

While her grannie saw her doctor, Meggie pulled out her laptop and got some work done. She was on her last email when a little boy of undetermined age came up to her and tried to pull the laptop from her hands. She looked around for his mother when the kid started screaming when she told him no.

"He just wants to play a game on it. Just let him and that'll be the end of his screaming." She didn't think that she'd heard the woman right and asked her to repeat herself. "It's not like you can't afford for him to have a little bit of time on it. What are you doing anyway? Playing games? He can do that, and you won't have to listen to him screaming."

"I happen to be working." She rolled her eyes at her, and the kid continued to scream at the top of his lungs. "Can't you entertain him? I mean, he is your kid, right?"

"I'm busy with my own stuff right now. And like I said, if you just give it to him, he'll be all right. It's something that keeps him entertained at home." She asked her why she didn't bring it with her to give to him when he got into this sort of mood. "Are you trying to tell me how to raise my kid? Listen here bitch, I'm doing the best I can without his daddy around. And since I know this baby daddy won't be around either, I'm going to be stuck all day with two kids screaming. Just give him the fucking computer and we'll all be happy."

"No. I won't." The nurse came out into the waiting room and told Debra to quiet her child. All she did was blame her for it, and the fact that she wouldn't give up her computer. The nurse rolled her eyes, too, and the child was smacked by the mother. Hard enough to knock him over and bust his mouth on the toys that had been left out for kids to play with. Now his screaming was twice as loud, and the mother was blaming her again.

"Ms. Rudy, your grandma would like for you to come back to her, please?" She gathered up her things, and Debra told her to leave the computer behind so that the rest of the room could get some relief. "Debra, keep him quiet, or I'm going to reschedule your appointment for eight in the morning again. I know how much you hate getting up in the morning."

Getting out of the room, once the door was shut, it was peacefully quiet. Going into the room with her grannie, she was told that she didn't really want her back there, but she thought that she'd save herself some heartache with Debra and bring her back. She was happy for it, but Grannie seemed confused about seeing her.

"Some mother in the lobby was disciplining her kid and blaming it on me. I'm sure that the little kid needs stitches. She just walloped him good." Grannie laughed and she smiled at her. "I don't know what's wrong with people these days. Thinking that they're entitled to anything someone else has simply because they want it. She wanted me to turn over my computer because she didn't want to deal with him."

She was glad that she'd been able to be there when the doctor came to see her Grannie. There were tests being set up for next week for her monthly blood work to be done, as well as her fasting for her diabetes test. She was able to schedule her grannie to come in at eight o'clock so she'd not be starving all day.

Glad that the doctor had put in the orders today, they were going to stop by the lab to get the other tests done, and not have to worry about them so early in the morning. Her Grannie didn't do well without her breakfast. It was to her the most important meal of the day. As soon as they left the office, she could hear Debra screaming at her son about crying all the time and blaming it on the lady who had stolen his laptop. Shaking her head, she invited her grannie to have dinner with her out.

"We should plan this every time you have an appointment. That way, we can end the day with a nice meal that no one has to clean up afterwards." Grannie told her that she didn't mind but would like a cheeseburger. "I would love one of those, too. With a bunch of fries and a milkshake for dessert."

They were pulling into the parking lot of their favorite place to get burgers when her cell phone went off. Not bothering to answer it while driving, she had her grannie answer. It was her business that she was running for her anyway, and if there was a problem, Grannie could handle it as well as she could. They'd been partners since her grandda had passed away several years ago.

"Yes, this is Ms. Ruby. What can I do for you?" Whoever it was made her grannie smile, and she wasn't going to take over when she was finally parked. "I don't know about all that, but I could have my granddaughter give you a call as soon as tomorrow.

I've been out of the business for a while now, and I don't know about mergers with another land deal."

Meggie nodded, telling her that there was a deal going on but didn't have the paperwork ready yet. Grannie rang off with the person and looked at her. They were ready to go and eat, so she waited to see what she had to say.

"You're buying the Pennington farm?" She said that she'd not heard anything about the Pennington farm. "That was the banker in town there. He said that he had it under good authority that the place was going to be on the auction block before too much longer. I don't know why, but I have a feeling that the man is lying to me."

"I could check on it. Do you know the Penningtons?" Grannie said that she'd known the grandparents of the boys who were trying to make a go of it. "How many boys are they, and are they boys to me or just to you?"

"To me. I'd say the oldest one is about your age now. There are five or six of them trying to make a go at the farm since their father had about run it into the ground oh, about a decade ago. I keep up with them without, of course, letting them know, but I don't think that they're behind in their taxes. Well, I know they're not. And I also know that the banker in town has a soft spot for all of them. He'd not just call up and tell you about this unless he had a reason. An auction? No, I don't see that being an issue with them." Grannie got out of the car, but she could tell that she was worried about it. "Could you have someone look into this for me? I will help them if that's the issue. Their grannie was a good friend of mine, and when she passed away not long ago, I told her I'd keep an eye on them for her."

"I'll do it right now." Pulling out her cell again, she made a call to Jackson, her private investigator. Asking the names of the men, she told him to do a deep file on the family and to let her know as soon as possible. "Also, look into an auction that might be going on there. And check out the bank for me. Something is fishy with that, too."

"The bank is run by a Mr. Peter Howard. He's a good man without anything in his closet. Also, I know for a fact that the Penningtons have kept up with their bills. I was in the station house this morning, looking into something else that was going on with a missing woman. I was told that the oldest, Kinsey Pennington, had reported what he'd overheard someone talking about the woman missing and a little girl who is now in protective custody. He'd gotten a loan from the bank to pay for some things around the farm. I asked and was told that even though they're struggling quite a bit, they're good men who have kept up with their taxes even when they have to do without." She asked about the loan. "He needed a hot water heater. I don't think that sounds like someone who is going to lose their house would do if they were broke. But I'll check into them and get back with you as soon as I find anything."

Grannie and her enjoyed their dinner, but they did talk about the elder Penningtons. Apparently, Grannie had gone to school with the elder Penningtons and had had a good, long relationship with them since then.

Chapter 2

Kinsey was just getting started on loading the milk containers on the big truck when he heard from the police again. They'd found the body of the woman who had been missing in the well on the back of the property. She'd been there for a few days, no more, but she'd been strangled and beaten to death. Tom had been arrested and was now awaiting a judge to come in and sentence him. There was no need for a trial as he had confessed to the entire thing. Kelley was now with her grandma, and it looked like she was going to be well cared for. He just didn't understand people. They treated their loved ones like tissues in a box. Use it and toss it away.

"Thanks for letting me know. The kid had an idea what was going on, I think the way she just told me that she'd been missing and her daddy was looking for her another momma." Officer Joseph said that was what she'd told them. That her daddy was out looking for another replacement for his wife. "Do you think she's going to be all right with her grannie? I mean, she seems like a good kid, but she's still only five years old."

"Mrs. Stocker is already raising one of her other grandchildren and seems to be doing a good job of it. The other little boy was clean and had a good smile on his face when we talked to her. She has the help of one of her daughters, who comes in and helps her with the boy when it gets to be too much for her. I did wonder about that, but I promised to keep an eye on them for a while anyway. Too many times, grandparents are raising their grandchildren for the parents."

He'd heard that was a big thing nowadays. Getting the truck loaded didn't take that long, and when the driver was gone with it, Kinsey went to the house to check on dinner. They were having pot roast again, and he wasn't going to let it get too dried out. He'd barely lived it down the last time. The house phone was ringing when he was going outside.

"Mr. Pennington, I'm assuming?" He said that he was one of them, but if he wanted to talk to any of them, they weren't at the house today. "I'll speak to you. I've been told that your family home is going to be auctioned off. Can you tell me if that's true or not? I've spoken with a couple of people about it, and they said that if you were auctioning things off, it was the first they heard of it as well."

"Who did you hear that from? We're doing just fine. Our taxes are paid up, and we own the land, so there aren't any liens against it or anything. I mean, we could have, I suppose, but we've never done that." The man said that was what he'd found out, too. "Are you finding this stuff out to be true, or are you just fishing to find out if you can get a good deal or not? The land isn't for sale in any way. I was just in the bank the other day and he didn't say anything about an auction."

"Well, I can tell you that we've heard that a member of the bank, we don't have a name as yet, has called someone on your behalf to buy the land. The firm that I'm talking about is called Ruby Gold. Have you heard of it?" He said that he'd not but knew of someone named Ruby. "That would be the family. Mrs. Ruby went to school with your grandmother and has been keeping an eye on your land for her. When she was called about the deal, she said that she didn't know that you were behind on any of your payments."

"We're not. Not at all." He asked the man who it was that he was working for. "I mean, you seem to know a great deal about us if you've heard about the relationship with Ms. Ruby and my grandma."

"I'm a private investigator who does work for the Ruby Gold company. As I said, Ms. Ruby was called about the auction and wanted her to have a heads up in the event she was looking to purchase some land. After getting off the line with a man who said he was with the bank in town, Miss Meggie called me and had me look into things. For her grandmother. I have to say I've never seen a better-looking family than yours, Mr. Pennington. There are no skeletons in any of your closets."

"While that's good to know, it doesn't really surprise me. We're all good men that are just trying to ink out a living by working our family farm." He said that he knew that, too. "Good. You can tell Ms. Ruby that we're not selling by auction or any other means. However, if we do sell out, and I'm not saying that we are, tell her she'd be the first to know. Grandma told us that when she was ready to pass on. She said that there were few honest people in the world, and Mrs. Ruby was one of them."

"I will tell her that, and thank you for giving me your time." He said it was his pleasure, but he did have work to do. "I understand. I'll get with my client and tell her what you told me. But if I were you, I'd see what I can find out at the bank. Someone said they were from there, and that was the reason this all started. Not Mr. Howard, by the way, but someone in there has it out for you men."

"I'll talk to Mr. Howard and see what he has to say about it." He would, too. Something like that kind of rumor could hurt them, and he was just getting ahead of the game here and didn't want some other person stepping in where he wasn't supposed to be.

"You have a good day."

After checking on dinner, he decided to go into town and nip this in the bud right now. Mr. Howard would know who was fucking around with their farm, or he'd find out. After getting cleaned up, he headed into town, leaving a note behind for his brothers that he'd talk to them later.

When Kinsey arrived at the bank, he told Mr. Howard everything he'd been told about the supposed auction and asked him if he'd heard anything.

"Not a word. And I'd be the first person who knew that something like that was going on. My goodness, if I'd have heard about that, I would have called you first thing. To think that someone was saying that they were from here bothers me on so many levels." Kinsey told him that he didn't believe it was him but wanted to make sure. "There was a man around yesterday who was asking questions about your farm. It never occurred to me that it might be someone wanting to cause trouble. I'll have to be more careful from now on."

"I'd appreciate it if you'd just let me know what you find out." He said that he would and wished him a good day. "I'll be at home for the rest of the day. Got some paperwork to fill out for seeds coming in, and it's my only day to get it done since it's raining today."

On his way home, Kinsey decided to go by the

realtor and ask about the land deals going on. While they had five thousand acres of land to use, they'd been renting out a good portion of it to other farmers for the last thirty or so years. The realtor handled the renters, and he would know firsthand, he thought, if there were rumors of an auction coming up for their farm. He didn't mention it, but he did have three checks for him for the rent.

Once he was on his way home, he decided to stop at the grocery store and pick up some pop-in biscuits. They'd go well with the roast he had on and make it go a little further with the gravy he was planning on making with it. There were already potatoes with it as well as green beans on the stove, simmering all day with hunks of bacon in it. Going through the line, he was surprised at how busy the place was for a Thursday. But then he realized it was the first of the month and social security checks had gone out.

Dinner was a huge hit this time, and he had enough leftovers to have hot-faced sandwiches later in the week. The biscuits had been really good at sopping up the gravy, and he was glad that he'd been able to make extra with the roast for them all. He missed Raphael at times like this, but he'd be home over the weekend, and that would call for steaks on the grill with him and baked potatoes that he'd been saving.

Since he'd served the roast in the same pot that

he'd cooked it in and the same with the green beans, there was little to clean up besides the plates. Since he'd done the cooking tonight, he didn't have to clean up, but he did finish the laundry. They were all enjoying the new hot water tank, and him especially. He could put in a load of towels to wash when he got up in the morning and not have to mess with them until he got back in the house that evening. It was really nice to have clean clothes too.

"I'm glad you got the garden in before all this rain. Made it easier not having to water everything." He said that he'd gotten the lettuce in several days ago and it was already popping out of the ground. "I noticed, too, that grandma's rhubarb is coming up nicely as well."

"I can't stand that stuff. I'll make some pies with it, but I'm not going to eat any of it. Tastes like slime to me." They made fun of him for doing all the baking and then teased him about how domesticated he'd become since getting out of the service. "They didn't teach me how to cook, morons, they taught me how to be a manly man."

Of course, they thought that was funny, too, and he laughed with them. He loved his brothers and would move heaven and earth for them, but there were times when he wanted to strangle one or two of them when they got to teasing him. He thought of himself as a manly man, and it had nothing to do with being in the service.

He was taking the trash out when he heard Wylie on the porch talking to someone. Not that he would eavesdrop on any of them, whoever he was talking to sounded like they were pissed off. As soon as his brother saw him, he hung up the call and told him that he needed to talk to him.

"We need to have a family meeting. Please?" He asked him what was going on. "I don't want to do this anymore, Kinsey. I'm sick of farming until we drop, only to get up and do it again the next day. I've not had a date in ages, and I want to be able to find myself a wife someday and raise a couple of kids while I'm still young enough to enjoy them." He sat down next to his brother on the porch swing.

"You never said anything like that before." He said that he'd been thinking about it for the last five or so years. "You were breaking a date off with someone. That's what I heard. Right?"

"Yes, and apparently for the last time. She's a nice woman, but sick of waiting for me to get my ducks in a row and not cancel another date with her. I've seen her a few times, but while I know she's not one I'd like to spend the rest of my life with, I can't get out of my head that she's out there and I'm missing her." He told him he was sorry. "Don't be sorry, Kinsey. I don't want that, but I have a feeling that the others are feeling the same way. I know that Gleason is sick of working for someone else when he's needed here. Bodi hates his job so much that he doesn't want to go to work anymore. And Ara said he's sick of working for a newspaper that doesn't pay him much and never having a story to sink his teeth into."

"I didn't know." He asked him if he missed dating. "I haven't thought of going out since I came back. I knew there was work to be done and put it on the back burner. Do I miss it? Yes. Very much so. I hate that the only time I get dressed up is for something to do with the farm and nothing that involves a soft woman. Like you, I have to believe that there is someone out there for us, but I've probably missed the chance of — is this because of the rumor and the auction?"

"No. Yes, a little bit. When I heard that it might be going on, I was excited to think that it might be a way for us to get out from under this place. Remember what grandma had to say? She told us to sell to the highest bidder and have a life. Right now, that sounds like a good idea." Not that he'd been thinking about all that much, but he did now. To be out from under the debt that would be coming to them in the fall again would be wonderful. And for him to go to work that offered insurance would be brilliant. Someone else to take over and do what he hated doing daily. "What are you thinking about?"

"How much I would love to leave the paperwork to someone else. That I'd love a job where when I got off at five, I was finished for the day." Stretching out his legs, he thought of what it would be like to have to sell this place off. "I'm sure that the renters of the land that we have would buy us out on what they're renting. But that wouldn't be enough, would it? You want out all the way."

"I do. It wouldn't matter to me if we just sold off everything and walked away. I do know that there are a lot of perks to us owning all this land. That we have meat when we want it. Fresh vegetables too. But even that doesn't stand up to us having money in our pockets and — selling this all would make us wealthy men, Kinsey. Wealthy enough that we could buy ourselves a home that was built in this century. A new car, as well as going back to college if we wanted, getting a better education for something that would keep us in money, and a new house." He told him that he'd given this a great deal of thought. "It's all I've thought about for the last decade. Okay, not that long, but about five years. I just want out. I'll stick it out if none of the rest of us want out, but I'm not going to be loving it anytime soon. I hate it here."

"All right. We should talk this weekend when Ralpheal comes home. He might not have an opinion either way since he's rarely around, but we all have to make the decision rather than one of us. It has to be all or none." He agreed with him. "All right. You tell the others, and I'll talk to Ralpheal when he calls tomorrow. Let everyone be thinking about it before Saturday."

Kinsey thought about it as he was getting ready for bed. It was barely dark outside when he was about ready, and he hated that as much as the others did. Getting up at the crack of dawn and going to bed early enough to be able to stay awake all day. There were other perks he knew that his brother hadn't mentioned, and he thought about those as well. Did he really want out of this as much as his brother did? He just didn't know.

Talking to Ralpheal the next afternoon, he thought that he'd not have an opinion, but he didn't want to live here anymore either. He wanted to buy himself his own home and settle down as well. That surprised him because he'd never said anything like that before, and he was also surprised at how happy he was to be coming home for this meeting.

He didn't even know how to go about selling this place. It was good acreage; the soil was good, and they had good yields when they grew wheat and alfalfa. Then there were the cattle that they had that they'd have to sell off as well. Or would it go with the farm? He didn't know. But he knew that if they did go ahead and sell off, he needed to talk to Ruby Gold. That was a promise that he'd made with his grandmother when she'd been dying. That he'd sell to her and only her.

"Don't you wait until you're as old as I am before you sell it off, Kinsey." He'd told his grandma that it was the family farm. "There ain't no reason for us to have a family farm if it's killing us off before our time. You sell it to the highest bidder, and you get out of this little town and find you a good wife and have a bunch of little ones."

The land was in his name only. The others knew that, so asking them if they wanted to sell out was just being nice. He'd split the money with them six ways, too. Just because someone had decided that he should be responsible for this place didn't mean that the others didn't have a vested interest in it being sold off. Before he left the house for the day, he put in a call to Ms. Ruby. He had her number in with the other things that his grandma had left him for when he was ready to get his head out of his ass, as she told him, and to sell the farm before it killed him.

~*~

Meggie didn't have time for sales calls today. She had three meetings today and four tomorrow. None of them were going to go well, she knew, especially if she was in the kind of mood that she was in now. When her phone beside her rang, she didn't want to answer it but knew that on some level it was her responsibility to at least say something nice to whomever called her.

"Ms. Ruby? Please don't transfer me again. I've been on the phone for an hour now, and I think I've been transferred at least a dozen times. I'm looking for Grace Ruby. I don't want to talk to a salesperson. I don't need anything looked into, I just want to talk to Grace Ruby." She told him that she was Meggie Gold, Grace's granddaughter. "Can you get me to talk to Grace then? I swear to you, I don't want to borrow money or pay for whatever a dividend is. Just talk to her."

"I can help you. My grandmother retired a few years ago, and I've taken on the job of talking to people who are looking for her. You tell me what you want, and I'll see where I can get you into the right department. Or perhaps to my grandmother. You tell me and I'll figure this out with you." He told her what his name was. "I know about you, Mr. Pennington. Your banker called here, telling me that you were going on the auction block for non-payment of taxes. I've since realized that was a lie and have been having a good talk with my grannie about your family. Especially your grandmother."

"My grandma told me that if I were to ever

want to sell the farm, I had to ask you guys first." She asked him if he was serious. "I am. At least I'm enquiring about it now. My brothers and I have been talking, and while we've not made a decision yet, I'd like to see what my options are for selling it all and walking away from this place. We're having a meeting together on Saturday when my other brother gets here, and we're going to talk it over. I thought that I'd get some numbers ready to see what sort of options we had here. We have a lot of acres to sell, and some of that is being rented to other farmers. Plus, I have about two hundred head of cattle, too."

"I'm to understand that you have about five thousand acres, correct?" He said that at last count, they did but one of his brothers was thinking of buying up the land next to them. "I'm assuming that it's part of the land that your father lost in his cards sometime."

"You do know a lot about us. Yes, our dad lost about three thousand acres about fifteen years ago when he was losing at poker. We've gotten most of it back, but for a few hundred of them, my brother has been looking into it. Farming isn't what it used to be. From what I'm to understand about our dad is that he was never any good at it and shouldn't have been playing the cards at all."

"Do you have access to a fax machine?" He told her that he did, and they had a landline in the house. "So do I in my own home. All right. You fax me whatever paperwork you have on your place, mineral rights, any renters' agreements that you have, and I'll get back with you on Saturday, if you'll allow me to be at the meeting."

"I'd have to ask my brothers. They don't know that I'm calling you yet. So you understand, right now it looks as if they all want out, but I think hearing what we can get for the place might be the kicker into it. Only my name is on the deeds. It was left to me when my grandma died. The others know that but have been helping me run the thing since we've been alone." He cleared his throat, and she could hear papers being shuffled around. "I have everything here. When we were able to get the land back from others around, it was put into my name as well. I don't know why we did it that way, but there you have it. If you give me a number, I can send this right over to you. It's about fifty or so sheets in case you have to load your paper up."

The fax machine started to work almost as soon as she gave him her number. It looked like he had the deeds first, then she was waiting for the other work to come through. While it was spitting out the papers that he was sending her, she began calculating what five thousand acres would be to the men. It was going to make Kinsey very wealthy, and if he split it six ways like it sounded like his plan was, they'd all be making a great deal of money off the sale of the land alone.

By the time the last sheet came out of the machine, she'd already figured out about how much was going to be coming from the sale of the place. In addition to the cattle sales and the equipment sales, there was a considerable amount of money coming from the sale of the house, too. Even if it was in poor shape, it would be worth a great deal as it was sitting in the middle of all the land that was prime selling land in the middle of Ohio and into other surrounding states.

Calling her grannie after getting an address from Kinsey, she told her what was going on. She was excited for the boys, as she continued to call them and hoped that they could broker a good deal for them. She told her grannie that she could sell the land to one buyer and be done with it, but she was going to put a for sale sign on it and let the highest bidder take it all.

"You won't divide it up?" Meggie told her that she didn't think she'd have to, that it would sell like it was. "Have you ever had a sale go for as much as this one is going to be?"

"No. Have you?" Grannie told her no, she'd not, but worried that people would be pissed about her not being a realtor. "I'm brokering a deal, not selling houses. Do you think that would make a difference?"

"I don't know love. But before Saturday, I'd look

into this to see if there are any rules about you doing this for them." She said that she would and was glad that she'd brought it up. "You look into it, and I'll ask around about things, too. I'm sure that the cattle will be nothing to get rid of. It's the house and the barns that might cause some trouble with people. If they want the land, then they might not care at all if there are houses and barns on the land. Understand?"

"I do. I'm glad I called you." She was making notes as her grannie told her things that popped into her head. There were other things, too, that she had questions about. Like, if it was all in Kinsey's name, why didn't he just sell it if he wanted out?

Meggie thought she had the answer to that. He was a good man, and his family was important to him. The numbers she was getting told her that all of them were going to be wealthy men if they decided to go through with this, and she'd make a bit off of it too. But she'd have to ask her grannie about that. Maybe they had a deal where all the money went to the Pennington family. Making a note to ask her about that, she dug into the paperwork and decided that she wanted to do this over everything she had going on today. It was something different from what she usually did, she told herself, and that was why she was having so much fun. Here of late, it was difficult for her to get her head into working because she was bored.

Meggie couldn't remember the last time she had a date. So long as she didn't count the men who would escort her to functions, it had been years. Usually, she would ask her foreman to go with her, but he'd gotten married last month and it took him off the market for her. Not that she was romantically involved with him, but he was a big enough man that others wouldn't bother approaching her if they were together.

She was bored out of her mind with the day-to-day work that she was doing. The same stuff day after day, and there was no end to the amount of paperwork that she had to shuffle around. Usually, it was just going over contracts for this or that company. Doing a buyout for another company or two. The place practically ran itself. She would swear that her secretary was giving her things to do so that she'd look like she was needed.

Later that afternoon, she told her grannie that she was going to go to the Pennington home for the family meeting. She asked her if she wanted to go, just to meet the boys that she'd only heard about. While she said she shouldn't go, Meggie could tell that she really wanted to and talked her into it—it didn't take much to persuade her to go, so she was happy that she'd not be going alone.

By the time Friday rolled around, not only did she have a better understanding of what had to be done to sell off the land that lay across five states, she had all the rules and regulations ticked off on which rules she could bend a little and which ones that she couldn't bend at all. Excited to be leaving the office for this trip, she even booked herself and her grannie rooms at the local bed and breakfast that was in town. There were even places that she wanted to go to while there and couldn't wait to take a little side trip to Amish country with her grannie. She'd heard so much about the place and she was going to make sure that she was able to get some much-wanted cheese and jerky. Oh, she just couldn't wait to get the meeting going, and then their trip to Berlin County for the rest of the day.

They were driving to the Pennington home, and she had a good idea of where she was going when she got out on the road. It wasn't a long trip, about forty-five minutes, but it was an adventure for the two of them. She had called before they left her house to see if the meeting was still on, and Kinsey told her that they were set to talk at noon. Would she be there?

"Yes, we're staying in town, so you can call me at this number and we'll come over. My grannie has come with me to meet you boys as she's called you forever." He said his grandma did the same thing even though they were all grown men. "Good. Then I'll see you when you call me. Thank you for this."

"No, thank you. I'll talk to you later." She felt

herself getting giddy with the upcoming meeting. She didn't even care if they decided not to sell. She'd had so much fun finding answers to questions she thought that they might have. It was going to be fun no matter how it turned out.

Chapter 3

Kinsey made up a veggie platter for them when the meeting was coming up. He knew his brothers well enough that they'd want snacks even though they'd just gotten up from the table. He even had some dipping sauce to use that he'd picked up at the grocery store. Kinsey was excited to get this thing started and find out what his brothers wanted to do.

Raphael said that he didn't feel like his vote should count as he was only home eight days a month. But Kinsey explained to him that they all voted, or it was off. He had to have an opinion on where he put his head when he was home, and he said that he didn't like the house anymore. Since grandma had died, it hadn't been the same.

"I agree. Nothing is the same since she passed away. Not even when I make some of her dinners do they taste the same when I use her recipes. I can get her sun tea to work for us, but that's not saying much. We only drink her unsweetened version of it, and that's not too hard to make." They both laughed. "Even just baking some sweet potatoes isn't the same."

"I do think you outshine her pot roast when you make it. Sometimes when I'm on the road and have to eat, I'll get some at the diner. I stopped trying to get one like the ones I have at home. They're nothing alike. Even the mashed potatoes aren't the same as yours. And they're just mashed potatoes." Kinsey thanked his brother for that. Then told him how he'd dried one out once. "I doubt that it was as bad as they said it was. They just like to tease you some. I know that I'd have eaten my share and theirs if they tried that when I'm there."

"We were having steaks on Saturday. Would you like a roast and all the trimmings? I have one in the freezer from the last slaughter." He told him that he'd love to have some with everything else. "All right, I'll get to that then. It'll be a good meal, and I'll even make some candied carrots to go with it."

"Now you've done it. I have to go for three more days before I can have what my belly has been craving all month. I can't wait to get home and taste it all. See if you can get the bread machine fired up, too. I'd love a loaf or two for myself with that gravy you make. Damn, but I want to come home right now and get it." He told him he'd make extra so that he could have some leftovers when he left. "You do that and I'll brain any of the others if they say a word about it too."

They didn't touch on the sale of the land

anymore, but he did have a nice talk with his brother. Sometimes when he'd come home, there were just too many of the others around to have a good conversation with each other because they all missed him. He and Raphael had become close over the years as he'd gone into the service at the same time he had. They didn't get into the same platoon, but they were able to see each other on other occasions.

That had been three days ago, and today he was getting dinner ready to be eaten before the meeting. When Raphael had come in last night, he'd been surprised by the loaves of crusty bread for dinner. He said that the bread machine could only make one loaf at a time, and he wanted that for himself. He thought the others would enjoy the crusty stuff.

Setting the table, everyone helped with putting it on the table. There were plenty of things for everyone to carry to the dinner table, and he was glad that he had spoken to his brother before assuming that he'd want steaks. The biggest hit looked like it was going to be the candied carrots, and he was glad that he'd made up a lot of them for today. Even the green beans had turned out all right, he thought.

The meal had taken him hours to make and only about fifteen minutes to eat. He always marveled at that when Grandma was cooking. Just how much time was put into a meal after planning it to be gone in less than a quarter of the time. But they were all full and content, and that's all he could have hoped for. There was plenty enough left over so that Raphael could take some with him to have a nice meal while on the road.

They never talked business at the table. That had been a hard and fast rule when his grandma had been alive. There was a place and time for everything, and at the dinner table wasn't one of them. Nor did they use cell phones either. Meals were meant for family time and not business. They had continued that well after Grandma was gone, and he loved that they did.

After cleaning up and getting the dining room set to rights, they decided to have the meeting in the dining room. Getting out the platter of vegetables, they were already digging into them even after saying how stuffed they were. It was then that he called Meggie to invite her and her grandma over. He hoped things went as well as he anticipated they would. Getting information was all they needed for now.

"If my vote counts for anything, I think that Kinsey should get double the shares of the sale. He's been holding this place together since he came home when grandma got sick." He said that they'd split things six ways or not at all. "I don't agree. I've been here with you the entire time, and I know how much you take on for yourself and don't tell us about. How long had the hot water heater been going out before you finally broke down and got one?"

"It had been a few months, but I was making it work." Wylie said that he knew that he had, and it had been great of him, but that was just what he was talking about. "I could fix it, that's all, and you guys would have had you been here when it finally broke down."

"I disagree, but I do agree with Wylie. Without you, none of us would have had a roof over our heads the way you've been keeping the wolves at bay around here. I know for a fact that I couldn't have gotten a job outside of this place without you holding up my end here. I know that it was supposed to be for the extra money coming in, but you'd never taken any of the money, so that was a bust." Ara looked at him as he continued. "You've done enough for this farm, Kinsey. To me, I'd love for you to sell it and keep the money, but I think we all could use some of it to start again. I want my own house, a wife, and some kids running around. As it stands right now, none of us is getting any younger waiting for the next bad news to take this all away. I think we should sell while you have someone to sell it to. And by that, I mean so that we can all enjoy the money while we still can. I don't want to be Grannie, god rest her soul, and hanging onto this place because it was called Pennington. She told all of us to make sure you sold it when a buyer came along, and I think you should do it. For all of us."

"It's not that easy." He went to the door to let in Meggie Gold and Gracie Ruby. After introducing them to his brothers, he sat back and let them do the talking. He was about ten minutes into her talking when he realized that it really was easy to sell it off, and they'd each be millionaires.

She had paperwork for them all. It told how the land was spread out over five states and that each state had rules about selling the land that was in their domain. There were prices that they could get for the cattle, both standing and butchered. There was even a chart on how much the house was worth, the way it was standing, or if they had improvements made to it.

"It wouldn't take much but time. It needs to have a new roof on it as well as a new furnace. I'd fix those things up before going to the market with it, just because it might make it worth more for the buyer." She explained how much those two things could cost and how much revenue they'd get back on the improvements. "The buyer might not even want the house there, so it's a gamble whether or not it matters to them. Even tearing the house down would give the buyers the option of building in the same place or not."

She talked for nearly two hours, answering questions and telling them things that the paperwork already had in it. Mrs. Ruby also had some input on the sale, telling them that she'd spoken to their grandma and she wanted them to sell. And why.

"She didn't want you to be raising any more Penningtons on this land. She said that she wanted the six of you to have homes of your own and money in your pockets." Mrs. Ruby laughed a little. "Your grannie had a good head on her shoulders about the farming industry. She said that it was a dying breed of men that could make it work, and she didn't want you six dying here like she did without anything to show for it."

"She had us to show for it." Mrs. Ruby said that wasn't what she meant. She meant for them to be able to move on from here. "What do you think this land will be sold for? I mean, what kind of buyers will they be that want this much land?"

"Mostly developers. And in that, they'd bring more businesses into the town. Everyone will benefit from the sale of this land, Kinsey. Not just you six, but towns across the state will as well. It will be a good influx of cash for a lot of people who live and work around here." He said he'd not thought of that, and his brothers agreed. How the town would be affected hadn't been brought up before.

"A developer would bring in construction crews that would eat and sleep in this town. I know that you have a few places that can accommodate people, but it would be a boon for the ones that are already here. The school will also benefit from the sale. There will be taxes paid to the town that will really do a lot for the local schools and other civic centers around here. Then it will only go up from there. New businesses. They'll hire locally, which will stimulate a lot of money in families' pockets. There is more, too." She explained how they'd more than likely get a grocery store that would be catering to the needs of the town. Car dealerships would come in, and cars would be there for the new money. "It's incredible what can happen if you decide to sell now."

They ended up ordering pizzas for dinner. He couldn't believe that they'd been talking for nearly six hours when he noticed the time. Inviting them to stay and have food with them, of course, they turned them down. They had plans tomorrow to go up to Amish country, and he thought that they were excited about that trip. He knew that he'd love to go, too, but didn't invite himself. They still had a lot to talk about. About the sale and the other things that came up while talking.

After the women left, they talked more into the night. There was a lot more that they had questions about that wasn't on the paperwork. Making notes on it, he knew he'd wait until Monday to talk to her so that they could have a good time on their trip.

"If we're taking votes now on whether or not

we should sell, I'm for it. I never realized how much it would help the town. I'm not thinking that it'll all be roses and daisies, but if we can get a new school out of this with a new football and soccer stadium, if nothing else, I think it would be worth it." Ara laughed as he continued. "We have the blessing of Grandma on this, and I think she was right in saying that she wanted us to move on and raise a family. While I'm sure that we could raise a family here, we'd be struggling for the rest of our lives, and that's not what she wanted for us to do."

They took a vote on whether they'd sell or not, and while they had some stipulations on the sale — more of the money going to him, they wanted to get out from under it while they were still young enough to enjoy the life that came from a big sale of the land. It would make them wealthy beyond any place they were now, and that's what they were looking forward to.

"I'm going to give you a sixth of whatever the amount comes to of my money. I want you to know that we all appreciate what you've done for us. And how, even though you're our brother, you never once said you were going to take it all and not give us anything." The others agreed with Raphael. "I love you, big brother, and I don't know what we'd do without you. That's about as serious as I can get right now. I have to go to bed to get some sleep before I have to pull out again tomorrow afternoon. Oh, and thanks for dinner. It was just what I wanted."

As the others slipped off to bed, he straightened up the dining room and went to bed as well. It was going to be a long day tomorrow, and he wasn't looking forward to it. He was going to be running on less than four hours of sleep when he usually had about eight. Yes, he thought tomorrow was going to be a long day, and it was going to be made longer by his thoughts about selling the land that they all had a vested interest in.

Waking when his alarm went off, he had three messages from Meggie. She'd forgotten to ask him when they'd be able to do this if they decided to sell things off, and did they have any questions about the sale that she might have missed going over. There was only the one thing, and he messaged that to her right away. He just hoped that she wasn't messing with their little vacation, worrying about them and their sale. It looked to him like it was going to go through. He was almost giddy with the fact that he was going to be getting out from under the farm.

~*~

Meggie parked her car in front of the massive cheese factory. This was the place that she wanted to visit more than any of the other places they'd been. Although they'd had fun at every place they'd been. She and her grannie had gotten lunch at one of the little diners along the main drag and were now so full they might bust before driving home. Of course, it didn't help that they'd eaten about their weight in fudge when they'd found a shop that dealt with a variety that seemed to defy anything that they'd ever seen before. Also, there were little shops that she'd picked up gifts for people that she was going to be hard pressed not to keep for herself.

"Have you heard from him since he messaged you at six?" She told Grannie that she'd not but wasn't expecting to. "I think they'll sell. And I looked over the paperwork that I had from his grannie, and there is no mention of us doing this for free. I don't know what the percentage will be on that, but it'll be a goodly sum."

"I've not put a price on anything yet, but I'm thinking that you might be right on them selling. They seemed kind of desperate about getting out and being on their own. I can't believe that they, all six, still live in that house. But wasn't it a pretty one?" Grannie told her that it was from love and care from the boys. "I don't know if you noticed it or not, but none of them are boys, Grannie. They're all good-looking men with good heads on their shoulders."

"I'm going to call them my boys from now on. I just loved the way they went out of their way to make sure that we had everything we needed. And that snack tray wasn't out there just for us. Did you see how the others tucked into it when they wanted? That Kinsey is a good-looking man, for sure. What did you think about him?"

"He's nice. And you can tell that he's been in the service. It's the way he talks and walks. I'm going to enjoy working with all of them." Grannie asked again about what she thought about Kinsey. "Are you trying to set me up with him? Don't bother. I'm more of a workaholic than he is. I'm betting that he wants a wife who will stay at home and cook dinner for him. Although I guess he can cook too. And keep a nice house. Have you ever seen a house lived in by six men so neat and tidy? I don't know what I expected, but it certainly wasn't the house that we went to. I at least expected there to be dirty socks lying about."

They both laughed as they made their way into the cheese factory. She made her grannie promise that she'd not buy any more fudge, no matter how good it looked. They were teasing one another when they got to the old-fashioned candy aisle. There were candies there that her grandma had grown up with, and they bought some of them for nostalgic reasons.

When her phone went off at two in the afternoon, she almost didn't look to see who it was. But when the Pennington name came up, she had to calm herself before she answered his message. Meggie didn't know why she was excited for them, but she really was. They'd be the right kind of men to get good use of the money they'd earned from selling off the family land. She didn't know what she'd do if she had that much land and wanted to sell it off.

"It's Kinsey again. He said that they all agreed and they want to sell. But they've also gotten a loan to get a new roof on the place and are going to wait on the furnace." She thought that was a good idea to get it done. "He said that they're going to do the roof themselves at a better cost and will have it done in a week. I guess they took your advice about getting a home improvement loan. I wonder if he told the banker what was going on?"

"More than likely. He'd want them to get the best price, too." She put two rolls of cheese in the cart they had and moved on to the jerky. Grannie and her were going to weigh a ton each if they didn't stop buying food while they were here. "I'm going to get myself a roll of Swiss. I'm going to have our cook make us some quiche and put them in the freezer so we can have them anytime we want. I so loved the taste of the one that we had for lunch."

Not only did they get a lot of cheese, but they also bought some herbal butter to go with the crackers they'd gotten. Grannie had picked up some spices that she wanted, and they soon had a nearly full cart of things. And of course, they got more fudge to take back. But she was going to put it all in a basket for the Pennington sale to give them as a gift for using her as their brokerage dealer. Grannie thought that was a wonderful way to gift them something.

"I've never done this before, but I want to with them. It'll be a good sale, I hope, and I hope soon for them. I have a feeling that as soon as it's put out there that it's for sale, then there will be a lot of buyers trying to get it cheap. I'm hoping that someone with a lot of free cash hanging around gets it instead of us having to split it up into sections. That would make them a bit more money, but it would take them longer to sell." Grannie asked if she had someone in mind. "Two men that I've dealt with before. They're forever asking if I ever come across a land deal, and this is a prime one."

"That little town is going to be in for a huge surprise when it's out there that they're selling. I think the little town depends on them to be around for a long time. Ara told me that the Penningtons have been on that land for over five generations. This is the first one of them to make a living at it. I guess their daddy wasn't worth a plug nickel." Meggie asked if she knew what happened to him. "He's in prison, last I heard. He accidentally killed his wife, he said in a drunken rage, and got life without parole. The boys were young then,

I'd say that Kinsey was eighteen when it happened. Last time I got to talk to their grandma, she told me that he's where he should be. And his kids are better off without him around."

"I don't know why, but I thought that he was dead. No one mentioned him when we were there. The land I know belonged to their grandmother, and she never left it to anyone but Kinsey. She is said to have thought he'd be the one who would sell it all and divide it up with the others." Grannie told her that he'd be the one that she'd depend on, too. Even when they were in the service. "Yes, he told me that they all sent their grannie money when they were away all those years. They're good men, and I hope they get what they want out of this. I surely do."

"I do as well. Like I said, this is the perfect time to be selling it off because they're young and have time to get with someone before they're too old and worn out to have kids." She had no idea why the thought of them having children depressed her so much, so she changed the subject. "What are we going to do for dinner, Grannie? Did you want to go to that all-you-can-eat buffet? I don't know about you, but I'm about snacked out for the day. I'd like some comfort food for dinner."

"That sounds wonderful. I don't know that I can eat all that much, but it would be nice to have choices.

I heard their fried chicken is the best in the state. And I want a slice of that chocolate silk pie that we overheard those women talking about at lunch. Doesn't just the name of it sound good enough to eat?" She said that she wanted some of the chicken noodle soup, too. "Yes, the noodles are made right there on the premises. I tried to make noodles once, and it was the worst mess I've ever made. I had flour up my nose for three solid days and thought I'd never sneeze right again."

She and her grannie had been laughing all day. It had been wonderful to get away, and she wanted to do more days like this with her. Her grannie was in her seventies right now and was getting around well. She didn't know what the future would bring and wanted to get as much time with her as she could.

After dinner, they decided to get a room for the night. It wasn't that far off until darkness descended on them, and she didn't want to drive while being so full. Buying them an extra-large cooler meant they could keep their stuff cold through the night. Plus, she wanted to have a big breakfast before they got on the road in the morning. It was time for a celebration. And the fact that she had gotten such a deal going made her feel like she was going to be doing something that would help people in the little town of Dresden.

Meggie couldn't sleep right away, so while her grannie was asleep, she pulled out her laptop and worked on the wording for the sale. She knew all the particulars about it, the acreage as well as the size of the house. Wanting it to be perfect, she even had pictures of the house and land sizes per state that she could incorporate into the sales pitch.

She did have two buyers that she wanted to give a heads up to, and she'd call them on Monday as soon as she got the contract to sell from the Penningtons. She didn't know how much interest the land was going to generate, but she was hoping for a landslide just for the men that she'd gotten to like.

Pulling up the background check she'd done on the men, there was no point in getting through all this to find out she'd made a big mistake with a few con artists. There, on the first one, was a picture of Kinsey Pennington in his uniform for the United States Army.

He had a boyish look about him. His hair was under his cap, so all she could see was that it was dark. Even with his pressed shirt on, he looked well-toned. The cords in his neck muscles looked delicious to her. Wondering where that thought had come from, she clicked out of the file and closed down her computer. Her mind was just tired, she thought, and she was exhausted and too full of sweet stuff for her to be thinking of men and their neck muscles.

Getting ready for bed, she thought of him a couple more times and got angry with herself for thinking of a man that she knew next to nothing about other than what she'd been able to pull up in a background check. Though it was really good, his check had been, she knew that he was just too perfect for what she'd been reading.

"There has to be a flaw somewhere on his body." Her face heated up when she realized that she'd been talking to herself, something that she thought she'd outgrown years ago. "Get him out of your mind, Meggie Gold, before you start putting him in scenarios that will get you into trouble."

Crawling into bed, she was determined to keep him out of her dreams. She was acting like a schoolgirl with her first-ever crush. While he was a really good-looking man, she knew that he'd be wanting her to quit her job and start being a stay-at-home wife. Something that she knew she'd hate.

But would she?

She'd thought about being just that when her parents were alive. They were forever gone to work when she was little, and she spent more time with her nannies than her own parents. Grannie was always there for her, but she wasn't the same as having her mommy and daddy around.

Grannie tried to make up for it by going to lunch and other fun dates with her, but it was never the same. Now that they were both gone, all she had were memories of them kissing her goodbye when they left in the morning and sending her off to bed when they got home. She was brought up with the knowledge that children were to be seen but never heard from. That rule had made her want to be a stay-at-home mommy when she had kids someday.

Someday she might want to do that, but for now she was happy enough — barely so at working herself into a frenzy. She wasn't even dating right now. There was plenty of time for that nonsense later when she had all her life set up the way that she wanted it. Any man that she married would have to understand that business was first until she had children, and that was one rule that she'd not break for anyone.

Chapter 4

Mr. Howard was the only one who knew about the sale and was having a good time teasing him about it. Kinsey had to admit that he was excited. Even doing the roof was fun, knowing that it was going to be keeping someone else's family dry and warm.

"Company coming." He looked over his shoulder and saw the big car pulling into the drive. He didn't know who it was, so he stayed on the roof with the other three. Whoever it was had to wait on them today. They were nearly finished with the roof, and if they had to come down off of it one more time, they were going to be a whole day behind again. As it was, they'd been working on it for four solid days now, and he wanted out of the hot sun.

"Mr. Pennington?" All four of them said yes, and the man looked like he thought it was funny for some reason. "I'm looking for Kinsey Pennington. I'm a courier for Ms. Gold. I have the signed contracts with me."

"I'll take them." Wylie was the closest to the ladder and went down to get the paperwork. "I'll just set them in the house on the table, Kinsey. That way we don't all have to come down and look it over again."

They'd been bombarded with paperwork since this thing began. Not that it wasn't important, the paperwork, it was just that there was a lot of it. They'd spelled his name wrong on the first one, and then the second batch of paperwork had left out Wylie. Since they were all going to benefit from the sale, he wanted all their names on the contract. This was the third set of contracts that they'd been given, and he hoped that they were correct. The man left them with the contracts, and they finished up the roof in record time, as it was going to rain this evening and they wanted to see if the place stayed dry inside.

Almost as soon as they were finished cleaning up the mess that had been made with the roofing, the skies opened up and the rain came down in what appeared to be buckets. They all stood on the porch and listened to the rain hit the tin roof and loved the sound of it. Kinsey even sat in the old rocker to enjoy the rain hitting the dry dirt while it flooded the yard with the much-needed rain.

"This will make the garden grow more." Wylie sat down next to him. "I saw that the lettuce was coming up nice enough that we could have a good salad off of it in a couple of days. Maybe we can have steaks tomorrow with a nice fresh salad." Kinsey just looked at his brother.

"Have you noticed that we talk about food a great deal? I mean, we can be getting up from the table, and one of us will mention that the next meal should be great. Why do you do that, you suppose?" Wylie said that it was about all he had to look forward to. "Well, that's about the saddest thing I've ever heard. Really? That's all?"

"Pretty much. I didn't even have that until recently. You've become quite the househusband. I do want to complain about my socks, though. They weren't mated properly." The other two teased him about their laundry, and he had a good laugh over it. He loved his brothers and was so happy that they were going to get to do this together. Selling off the land was going to hopefully make them closer still. "But seriously, we're all going to have to learn some of the food recipes that you've been cooking so that we can impress our wives when and if we ever get one."

Going to bed that night, he had to be careful of all the little cuts he'd gotten from the roof installation. He'd not thought of gloves when he'd started out and had cut his fingers up really badly. All of them had. By the second part of the day, they were all searching for heavy gloves and wearing bandages to keep the cuts from bleeding through. But the roof was on, and they didn't have to worry about it any longer.

On Monday, just three days from now, the farm was going live, as Meggie called it. There would be lots of signs posted both around the land and on every site that had to deal with the sale of farmland. Meggie told them that they'd be overrun with people trying to get a better deal than had been advertised as well. He was both nervous and terrified about it. But deep in his heart, he knew that with all the plans they'd been making about the sale, it wouldn't sell. He just knew that there wasn't going to be any interest in the place at all, and they'd gotten all this work done for nothing.

Kinsey didn't tell his brothers that. But he had a pretty good feeling that they were thinking the same thing. That their plans of having their own home and family somewhere else were going to be for nothing. Not that they couldn't have a family, but they'd be raising them on the Pennington land the same as he'd be doing. Some nights, he went to bed feeling sick about his thoughts. There wasn't anyone that he could talk to about it either.

Milking the cows the next morning, he tried his best not to think about anything. Finally, after getting the milkers going and having had enough of his gloom and doom thoughts, he called Meggie. He'd been talking to her off and on for the past month, and he thought that she'd be honest with him if he asked her about the sale. For all he knew, she could be having the same feelings, that they were all getting their hopes up too far, and nothing would come of it.

As soon as she answered the phone, he could tell that something had happened with her. He thought he knew her well enough to know that she'd been crying too. After getting her to tell him, all she did was sob about how she wasn't having a good day and that one of her foremen had quit because he'd gotten a better-paying job somewhere else.

"I could have given him more had I known he was looking. I'm not a monster." He said he knew that. "I didn't even know he was looking. He's been with me for ten years, and this other company is giving him more money and a better position. I could have done that. He only had to tell me that he was thinking of leaving."

"You're a good boss. It's all on him leaving you. That's sort of a shitty thing to do, to up and leave you like that. Did he at least give you notice?" She told him that he'd not. That his job was there only if he took it right then. "Well, something is up with that. No one would want a person to leave without giving notice. They'd not want that to happen to them, I'm sure of it. Yeah, I'll say it again, that was a shitty thing to do to you." Her little laugh caught him off guard.

"You would be nice to me. I was just getting ready to call you when you dialed me. What did you want now that I've sobbed all over you about my day?" He told her that it didn't matter now. He felt better about the sale. "Are you worried about the sale? Don't be. I have three people right now waiting for it to go live so that they can put in the first offer. It'll sell if that's what you're worried about."

"My brothers and I have all these plans that we're going to be doing with the sale. I know we shouldn't have done that, but it's hard not to know what to do with the money when it sells." She told him that even bringing in a realtor wasn't going to take that much money from them. "Oh, we're not worried about the money. You've made it clear about what we'll make if the sale goes through. I'm worried that it's going to be years and years before it sells *if* it sells."

"You need to be more positive." He told her that he was positive that it wasn't going to sell. "You're silly. I promise you that as soon as I have someone on the line to buy it, I'll let you know. I don't think you're going to be unhappy with any amount that it ends up being. This is going to put you six on the map and me with a bit of money too. I've been thinking about my end, too."

"I guess we'll know in about three days whether or not we're going to be working the land for the rest of our days or not. Even Raphael is coming home early tomorrow to be here when it sells. They're all that confident. I think." She asked him if he thought his brothers were doing the same thing that he was doing. "I don't know, to be honest. We haven't been talking about the sale at all. I mean, a question will come up, but that's about all. If nothing else, we got a new roof on the house, and that made it worthwhile."

"I can't believe that you're not positive about this. I would have thought that you'd have a list made out of what you're going to buy first." He made himself not glance in the direction of the list he'd made up about what he was going to do with his part of the money. "I have one. It's not as extensive as yours should be, but I'm making one. I'm going to buy myself a house that I love. Not that I don't love the one that I'm in, but I grew up in the place, and it doesn't hold any kind of mystery for me. Grannie said that I need something larger. It only has the three bedrooms in it and they are being used by us, and one as my office."

"If I had a list, and I'm not saying that I do, I'd have a new truck on the list. My grandda bought the one that I've been using new thirty-five years ago. It runs when it wants to and stops the same way. I love that he had it new, but I really need something reliable that I can use in the winter months. With my new house." They laughed. "I have silly things too that I'd like to have. Like new socks and shirts that don't have more holes in them than are necessary."

They went on about what they'd buy, silly things that they'd get if the sale went through. By the time the call was an hour old, they were both laughing hysterically and having a good time. He was really glad that he had called her when she said that she was glad that he had.

"It was my pleasure. I do feel much better. I'm not sold on the land selling yet, but I do feel much better just talking to you." He had been wanting to ask her out since this entire thing started, but didn't want to be turned down by her. He was just getting the nerve up when she spoke again.

"How about we have dinner sometime? Just the two of us and no talk about the sale." He said that he'd love that. "I would as well. Just two people who have had a good laugh together, having a good meal. Someplace that sells seafood. I'm sure you told me once that you love seafood when you can get it."

"I would love that. I can eat my weight in crab legs. When I was out of the country, I would go to this little restaurant that served them on Friday nights. A bunch of us would go there when we got paid. I think they might well have hated it when five of us would show up for all-you-can-eat meals." He laughed at the memory. "There was this place that served Chinese too that we'd hit up. Oh the memories I have of that place."

"Grannie and I went to the buffet up in Amish

country. I think that I put on ten pounds while I was there. All right. Friday night, the night before we go live, you and I will have dinner and have a lovely evening." He said that since she knew where he lived, she could pick him up. "I'll do you one better, I'll send someone to get you and we'll have a wonderful time. I know just the place we can go to. My treat."

"It'll have to be. I'm broke, remember?" They both laughed again, and he told her that he could get to her house. After getting the address, they hung up. Kinsey hadn't realized how long he'd been on the phone until Wylie came back in to find him. He thought that he'd fallen or something.

"Just talking on the phone." He asked if it had been Meggie. "Yeah, it was. Why do you ask? I mean, you're all right with that, aren't you?"

"I had hopes that the two of you would hang out together. She seems perfect for you." He felt his face heat up when he told him about the date. "Good for the two of you. I'm so happy that you guys are going to get together. I mean, it might not be long-term, but it'll be nice if it is. You'd be the first of any of us getting what we all desire."

"It's just a date. I doubt that she'd want to have anything to do with me after the sale goes through. As I said, it's just a date to get some seafood." Wylie just nodded at him and walked away.

Kinsey then looked at the list that he'd been making while on the phone with her and laughed about the things that he'd ended up putting on his list. In addition to new socks, he'd put on it a suit too. Something he'd not had since he'd graduated from high school. Even then, it had been second-hand.

Going back to work, he was deep in fixing the tractor again when he noticed that it was getting late. He'd not put any dinner on because everyone was going to get their own, so he realized that he should have done something for himself. As soon as the tractor fired up and was going, he got on it to plow around his garden. It was much larger than it had been last year and even the year before. He wondered if they'd be here when it was time to harvest it. The least he could do was have the peas that had come on early. That was what he was going to have for his dinner. A nice pot of peas with cream sauce with them.

After his dinner, he finished up the paperwork for the roof. They'd had to be certified on the laying of it, or it would have nullified the warranty. There were still things that he needed to keep up on, one of them was the billing for the milk, and he had to make sure that even the Amish that he'd been working with knew of the potential sale of the cattle. They were going to sell them off at the end of the sale unless the buyer was going to take them on, too.

It was a little after ten when his brothers came home. He could have joined them, but he decided that he didn't want to be with a crowd tonight. Wylie had brought him home a piece of cheesecake that he'd gotten for him, and he sat and ate it while listening to his brothers being brothers. He knew that he said this a great deal to anyone who would listen, but he was proud of his brothers and thought they were good men, dependable men too.

Going up to bed later than he normally would, he looked in his closet to see what he had to wear on a date. Nothing jumped out at him, so he hoped that his newer jeans and shirt that he'd gotten for Christmas one year ago were enough. He'd even polish up his shoes before going to dinner tomorrow night and was smiling as he dug around in his closet for the box of shoe polishing stuff. It was right where he'd used it the last time, when his grandma had passed on.

He'd been thinking about her a great deal over the past few weeks. She'd been a good mother to them all. Even when he'd joined the Army, he'd made sure that she had money when he did. All of them, he thought. Each of them was doing their stint for the country; they'd all graduated from high school and gone straight into the service to get their college paid for.

Ara was the last to graduate from college with

a degree in journalism, going part-time until he got it finished. He'd taken six years to get his degree in husbandry, thinking that it would do him more good than not. It had served him well over the years, but he did wonder what he'd do with all his knowledge after the sale. Kinsey thought that even if he was able to get himself a new home out of this, he might well have a couple of cattle and a garden. Then thought that he was just getting back into what he'd been in before.

Going to bed at eleven, he knew he was going to regret it tomorrow. But he also had something to look forward to, and that kept him on pins and needles. As soon as he laid down on the bed, he realized that he was going to get to sleep soon and rolled to his back to turn off the lamp. It was the last thing that he remembered before the alarm woke him up in the morning.

~*~

She'd been calling it 'the date' since she asked him out. Meggie didn't feel bad for being the one who did the asking. She was about as excited as she'd ever been about going out with someone. As soon as she figured out what she was going to wear, that was.

Knowing that he'd not be dressed up, she downplayed her own outfit. Twelve times now. Her room looked like a tornado had gone through it, and there were hangers and outfits everywhere. She was dressed in a pair of slacks and a sweater when her doorbell rang. Looking in the mirror, she decided that she could always change again if he was dressed better than her. Going to the door, she was never so excited as she was then about having a man take her out to dinner. Or she him. They'd play that part by ear, she supposed. She opened the door to hear him talking to the gardener.

"No, I'd not pull them up until I was sure that they weren't going to be coming back. Those don't look as dead as I think they could." She looked at her gardener and asked what was going on. "Nothing. He was saying that he was going to have to pull out the rose bushes this year, and I told him I'd just trim them to the ground and wait for them to grow back in. We have the same kind of roses around Grannie's grave and do that every year so that they don't get out of hand." She'd forgotten that he had a minor degree in herbs and would know a little about the plants that were around.

"You look fantastic." She felt her face heat up when she said that sort of loudly. "I'm sorry. I've been debating all day on what to wear, and I was worried that I'd be overly dressed. The restaurant doesn't have any rules about what to wear, and I'm glad that you didn't go all out in a suit."

"I'm going to get one when this is finished. I want to be able to date and look better than a farm hand when I go out." For some reason, that bothered her that he was going to be going out with someone else when he sold the farm. Asking him to come in, Grannie wanted to talk to him, and he came into the house and made her otherwise large entryway look smaller by comparison. "You're a big man, aren't you?" She told herself to shut her mouth as she was just blurting out anything that came to her. "I'm sorry. You must think I'm terribly rude. I'm so sorry."

"I think that we're good enough friends that we can say what we want." He handed her some flowers that she'd not noticed until then. "These are from the garden around the house. I thought that I'd bring a bit of the farm to you and then we'd not talk about it again. All right with you?"

"No one has ever brought me flowers before." She felt her eyes fill with tears. "It's been a stressful day, and this is simply the best thing that you could have brought me. I remember seeing them when Grannie and I were there." She took them to the kitchen and was glad that he followed her. "I'll have them put in a vase for tomorrow's dinner party. Grannie is having a few of her friends over for bridge tomorrow night."

She didn't want to drive to the restaurant, so they took the service that she used to go. This allowed them to talk about things, and they were both really good at not bringing up the sale. She loved how they could talk about anything, and he was up on the topic. She never thought that he was stupid or dumb, but she'd been on dates — a long time ago — where the men would just grunt when she brought something up, and this was a wonderful change.

As soon as they were seated, he ordered a bottle of wine for the two of them. He said that he'd been joking about being broke and could afford dinner. She laughed; it was funny to her that he was so free with her that he could bring something like that up and not be embarrassed about it. She really liked this man and hoped they could see more of each other in the future before he found his perfect wife and left her out in the cold. Meggie was being silly, and she knew it, but it was painful to her heart to think that he'd be finding himself a wife before too much longer and no longer her friend.

They talked about so many things, and she was happy for it. Kinsey seemed to be well-versed on the topic of brokerage firms, and she answered him when he had a question. No topic was taboo, but the sale, and she thought that they'd done really well until dessert was served.

"I hate to bring this up, but what will happen tomorrow?" She told him that she didn't expect anyone to call on the first day, really. "I thought that your phone would be ringing off the hook with questions about the place."

"People will need to be looking into the sale. Even though there is a description about the land and the sale, people will still need to investigate it. See if there are any leans on the place, things like that. And as I said, even though it says that there aren't any people will need to make sure. I'm not saying that there won't be any calls, people will be calling about the price per acre as well as what sort of rights are on the land. The renters have all signed an agreement that they'll give up the land if it sells, but they would like to be able to buy the acreage that they've been using all these years. I had no idea that people rented farm land for so long. One of the renters told me he'd been renting the land for three generations. That's unheard of, I think."

"My grandparents were big on helping out the other farmers around. We weren't using it, and for a while it didn't look like we were going to be able to keep it, thanks to our father, but the rent coming in has been great for us since it comes in monthly." She asked him if they'd complained to him. "None of them have. One of them actually told me that he's been waiting for us to sell out for some time now. At least since grandma died. She was in touch with all the people of the town all the time."

It had rained during dinner, but it was beautiful after they were finished. The night had cooled off a great deal, so they decided to walk around the little town and have an ice cream. She loved ice cream more than she did meals sometimes. When she brushed her hand against his, he took her smaller hand into his larger one and held it. She could have jumped to the moon and back, she was so happy.

Inviting him back to have a nightcap at her home seemed the next step. She didn't have any illusions about them jumping into a relationship, but she was happy when he agreed to come back with her. As they sat in the back of the car on the way back, he pulled her into his arms and kissed her. Something that she'd been thinking about for a week, at least since she'd asked him out. He pulled away and looked at her.

"I don't know what this is going to do, this sale, and I'm happy for it. But I'd also like to see you again. After the rush." She said that she'd like that, and he smiled. It was the first time that she got a good look at his eyes as they stared back at her. "You're a very beautiful woman, Meggie. I'm excited to be able to see you on a more personal basis."

"I am as well." She cleared her throat and looked around the car they were in. "I guess this isn't the best place to say this, but I was wondering if you'd like to stay the night. I've been thinking about us...hopefully us having some fun before everything happened."

"I'd like that very much." He shifted in this

seat and turned to look at her. "As I said, you're a very beautiful woman, and I'd be thrilled if we could take this to the next level or whatever it's called." His laughter made her smile. "In the event you didn't know it, I'm about as nervous as a boy on his first date with a woman."

"Me too." She moved closer to him and smiled again. "I don't sleep around. In fact, I had to think when the last time I'd had sex with someone. It's been a while."

"Myself too. The last date I was on was when I got home from the service. I've seen other women, but nothing that would be considered a date." She stared at him, and he laughed. "I don't sleep around either, just so you know. I'm really fucking this up, aren't I?"

"No. One of the things that I really like about us is that we can be honest with each other. If that means that we get embarrassed, then that's all right too. At least we're being up front with each other and have no expectations about anything that might go on with us now and in the future." Kinsey pulled her into his arms again and kissed her.

The kiss was possessive and hungry. When he moved her again, she felt a cool breeze over her breast and looked down at herself. He was suckling her nipple even as she realized that he'd undone her top and exposed her. Christ, she wanted him more than she had any other man she'd dated before.

Moaning when he pulled away from her, his breathless muttering that they were at her home had her pulling her top back up and adjusting herself. She could have had him right then, but for him keeping an eye out for where they were. If he'd not been paying attention, there is no telling how far they would have gone in the back of the car with each other.

After he got out of the car, she was handed out by him. She could tell that he was hard; his cock was right in her face when he helped her get out of the vehicle. The thought of taking him into her mouth right then had her face heating up so hot that she was sure that he could feel it. This was the perfect way to end their night, and she was never so happy that he was going to be spending the night with her. God only knew what they'd get up to in her bedroom.

Chapter 5

Her grannie was up when they got into the house. Kinsey was trying his best to behave himself and keep his stone hard cock from misbehaving too. After talking to her grandma for a few minutes, she said she was headed to bed and would see them in the morning. It was as if she knew that he was spending the night with her granddaughter and giving them her blessing. Blessing or not, he was ready to throw Meggie against any hard surface and have his way with her. Groaning to himself, he knew that those sorts of thoughts weren't helping him behave.

"Would you like a drink?" He nearly screamed at her that he would love one. Anything to calm down the mood. "I want you to know that I've never invited anyone to my house before. I don't want you to think that because I really like you, Kinsey."

"I like you too. A great deal." She took his hand as they headed into the living room. There was a bar in the room, and she poured them both a whiskey. He had to remind himself that he couldn't gulp it down to calm his nerves, but laughed out loud when she did that very same thing. "I was just thinking of doing that."

"I'm nervous." He told her that he was as well. "Good. At least we have that in common. Actually, we have a great deal in common when you think about it. I will admit that I had hopes of you spending the night." She put her hand to her forehead and looked distressed. "My room is a mess. I'm going to run upstairs and put it to rights right now."

"I'll help. You should see my room. It took me hours to figure out what to wear, and my room probably looks a great deal like yours does." He stood up. "Come on. I'll help you and we'll have it set to rights in no time."

He couldn't believe how much he wanted her, but now that they were in her room—it was a disaster—he felt calmed by this normal thing to do. As he helped her hang her things back on the hangers, they talked about how much they had in common. He'd not realized it before, but was glad for it.

After the room was cleaned up, he sat down on the edge of the bed with her. She didn't look as nervous as she had before, and he was feeling calmed by her just being with him. Two things occurred to him at once. Before he could voice his concerns over his lack of preparedness, she sat on his lap, facing him.

The kiss was tender, and he wanted more of it.

More of her. As he slipped his hands down the back of her blouse, he pulled free the pins in her hair. When it came tumbling down on his hands, he reached up and curled his finger in the curls that were there. He pulled back enough to look at her with her hair down around her shoulders.

"Beautiful. You're simply beautiful."

Her top came off much easier for him than it had in the car. Her bra was a bright pink color, he'd not seen that in the darkened car, and he made his way with his mouth down to the plumpness being pushed up and out of it. Getting her bra undone, he was thrilled when she curled her own fingers in his hair and held him to her. Her breasts were well-formed and delicious. He couldn't wait to taste more of her.

Rolling her to her bed, she moaned when he slid his hands down to her ass and squeezed the muscles there. Pulling her closer to him, he nearly came when she rolled her hips up to meet his downward stroke. He wanted her naked now and moved to stand up when she told him she had condoms.

"I don't want you to think that I have them for just any encounter. I told you that I wanted you." Kinsey told her that he'd thought of that too late and was glad that she had. "I was a Girl Scout." That, of course, had him bursting out laughing.

Standing up, he was pulling his belt from his

pants when she started at his pants button. When her fingers brushed over his cock, he couldn't hold back the moan if he tried. She finally got the snap open and had his zipper down when he was going to reach for the condoms in her drawer. However, the moment she took his cock head into her mouth, all was lost for him.

"Christ, that's wonderful." She pulled his pants down to his thighs with his help. Holding her head over him, he fucked her mouth as gently as he could. Which he thought was still too hard. When she pushed him back and stood up, he pulled his pants the rest of the way off while toeing off his shoes. When she told him to hurry, he wanted to just rip them from him, but knew on some level that he needed to have something to wear home.

She was naked before him when he finally got his pants off, and was naked too. She looked glorious to him, and he wanted to savor this moment for a little while. But she was touching him again, making his own nipples as hard as hers were, and to taste her like she had him. Pushing her back on the bed, he got down on his knees after spreading her legs wide and looking at her nectar before him.

"I want to eat you. Are you all right with that?" For an answer, she laid back on the bed with her arms beneath her. Leaning into her pussy, he nearly came again when she flooded his mouth with cream. Her climax took his breath away, and he found that it wasn't nearly enough of her. He wanted her all.

Curling his tongue around her clit, he lapped at her while she came a second time. They weren't what he wanted; he wanted to come with her, but knew that he had to work up to it. He was a large man, something that he'd forgotten to mention, and didn't want to hurt her.

Kinsey fucked her pussy with his tongue, and when she gave him what he wanted, more of her cream, he slid his finger into her and fucked her that way. When she cried out his name, all he could think about was winning the prize at the end of the game and fucked her more. She was beautiful lying this way with her legs spread out and her hands on her breasts.

He watched as she played with her breast, teasing her nipples that he'd tasted. When she licked the tip of one, he nearly cried out for her to do it again. Watching her, forgetting the task at hand, he nearly missed when her hips came up off the bed in the most beautiful climax he'd ever seen a woman have. Making sure that he caught every drop of her release, he put his hand over his cock and masturbated himself while she cried out again that she was coming.

When she reached for him, it was all he could do not to plow her. He wanted so badly to be deep inside of her right then. Reaching for the condoms that were still in the dresser, he fumbled around with it until she took it from him and helped. But first, she took him into her mouth again and swallowed him beyond the tight muscles in the back of her throat. He couldn't have held back his release if he had to.

Fucking her mouth, he nearly came a second time when she let go of his cock with a small popping sound. Looking at her over his body, all he could think about was that she was his and forever. After the condom was rolled over his cock, she sat up over his groin and took him deep inside of her. It was all it took for him to come, seeing her riding him like she was, had been all it had taken for him to lose control once again.

Neither of them said anything while he got up and dealt with the condom. Getting back in bed, under the covers this time, he held her in his arms and liked the feeling. Closing his eyes, only going to rest for a few minutes, he wrapped his arms around her warm body and fell asleep.

Waking up to a darkened room, he didn't know where he was. It wasn't until Meggie touched him that he understood that he was in bed with her. Asking her if he should leave, she giggled a little and told him no, she had plans for his body in the morning. Of course, that's all she had to say, and he was hard again.

Making love to Meggie was soft and wonderful.

They took their time in getting to know one another's bodies, and he loved the way her body fit against his. Her breasts were just a mouthful for him, and he loved how her nipples would get hard in his mouth. Everything about this woman had him wanting to make love to her for the rest of his life.

The condom gave him no trouble the second time. He was careful with himself; he didn't want to come before he'd brought her several times. But almost as soon as he was deep inside of her, she came twice, crying out his name both times, and he loved the sound from her beautiful mouth when she did.

Making love to her while she came twice more, he felt himself empty inside of her and promptly fell asleep. It was hard on his body having come so many times, and he found that he couldn't stay awake for very long. However, he did get up a few minutes later to use her bathroom and was glad that she'd gotten more than one condom. At this rate, they'd be using the entire box in one night. And he found himself not caring one bit.

When he woke up, it was nearly five in the morning, and he slipped out of bed to get a quick shower. He was feeling kind of sore from making love all night and knew that if he had to work right now, he'd be too sore to do much. Getting his clothing gathered up, he was surprised when she said his name.

"I was going to leave before your grandma got up." She told him to come back to bed because she wanted to sleep in. "Will she not care? Because if it were up to me, I'd not leave at all."

"Come to bed. I'm too sore to do much more than just let you hold me." He took off the clothing that he'd gotten on and got into bed with her. "I could get used to this. Having you in bed with me has made me realize that I've gone too long without the right man in my bed."

"Why, thank you, ma'am." She curled herself around him again. "I will have to go home sooner rather than later. I have a lot of work to get done. Especially if the sale isn't—where are you going?"

"The sale is today." He said that he knew it, he'd just said that. "I want to see if there are any calls to see about it. We should both go down and get some breakfast anyway. I feel like I could eat an entire cow right now."

And just like that, she was in the shower, and he was left getting dressed. Laughing to himself, he wondered what Wylie was thinking about him not being at home, and thought that he didn't care. He was a big boy and could stay out all night if he wanted. But he did text him to let him know he'd be home later in the afternoon. There was no point in making him too worried about him. His message back was champagne glasses clinking together. Leave it to his brother to embarrass him online.

He didn't know if he should go down to the kitchen or not since Meggie was in the bathroom. He also didn't know if she would take a longer shower than he had or not. There was a lot of stuff he didn't know about her, but was willing to learn. He was in the kitchen when the cook asked him what he wanted to eat.

"Whatever Meggie eats, I'm fine with that." She nodded once and went to the refrigerator. He sat down at the bar in the room and asked if he could help. "I can cook too if you have other things to do."

"I'm going to cook you a big breakfast, young man. Now all you have to do is tell me how you want your eggs and we'll be just fine." Grace came into the kitchen then, and she was dressed up. "The ladies have all confirmed that they'll be here at six on the dot, mistress. I hope that's all right."

If they were going to act like it was all right with him being there, he was going to be all right. It wasn't until Meggie came into the kitchen and kissed him that he felt like he was a part of the house. She told her grandma that she'd gotten two calls already and that she was hoping for several more.

"What happened to David Winchester and his need for land? Surely you told him about it." She said she sent him the same flyer as she had sent to everyone else. "Good. That man is going to own a couple of states before too much longer. Did you tell him that the land is over — of course you did. You would have told everyone that. More bang for their bucks."

They talked around him. Mostly about the upcoming dinner tonight, but about the sale as well. When a platter of food was set in front of him, he was sure that he was required to share it. But when Ms. Maple, the cook, set one in front of Meggie, he had to smile. She must have thought that they worked up a hell of an appetite last night. And after his first bite, he thought that he had as well.

It was nearly noon when the calls started to come in. Meggie said she was surprised by that but didn't say it was a bad thing. When Mr. Winchester called her, she told him everything that had been in the flyer about the land and even asked him a couple of questions about the land. Like, did the house come with it. He had to ask himself, what would he do with the house if he sold the land under it. But he did ask only himself, not wanting to make a fool of himself.

When she said that she had to go to the office, he decided that he should be starting home. He had plenty of work to do and didn't want to leave it all on his brothers. As soon as he got into his truck, she came out of the house to talk to him. Turning off the motor, he smiled at her when she pouted prettily, telling him that she wished that he could stay.

"I'll call you tonight. And when I have some good news." He told her that he'd keep his cell phone on him. "All right. I wish you could stay today, but I know that you have work to do."

"Wylie will have started on it, but it'll take the two of us to get all the work done today. Ara is coming over this afternoon, too." She smiled at him and told him she'd enjoyed their time together. "So did I, but I will only admit this to you, I'm sore in places that I've never been sore before." They both smiled at his admission, and she said that she was as well.

Driving home, he thought about the night he'd spent with Meggie and was glad for the time they had. Now, if the land were to sell, he'd have more time for things like this with her, and nearly turned around to go back to her, thinking fuck it and letting his brothers take care of the day. But he didn't, knowing that he'd feel guilty about it.

He was pulling into his driveway when his phone rang. Since he didn't know the number, he let it go. Whoever it was, they'd leave a message if they wanted to talk to him, and he wasn't going to let his good mood go because of a phone call. Wylie was waiting for him when he got changed and made his way to the barn.

"Everything all right?" Kinsey told his brother that things were just fine, and they set to work. He did ask him about the sale if they'd heard anything, and that was about it. Telling him that Meggie was going to call if she heard anything seemed to be all right with him, and they continued with their jobs in getting the cows milked and the milk ready to be transported to Berlin.

At four, they quit for dinner. It was early, but he'd not eaten anything since breakfast and was starving. There was just enough leftovers for the four of them to have open-faced sammiches, and there was plenty of tea for them to have with it. Setting up the tea maker to make some more for the four of them, they ate the rest of the cake that Ara had picked up at the day-old grocery store for their dinner. He didn't see anything wrong with it and was happy for the sweetness after having a big dinner. Exhausted now, he made sure to keep that to himself while they finished up the rest of their chores after dinner.

Kinsey had forgotten to check his phone for messages after the call that had come in. The person had left a voicemail. Getting a pen and paper to write it down, his phone rang, and it was Meggie. Smiling for the first time all day, he thought, he greeted her with his usual charm and laughed when he realized that he didn't have shit as charm anymore.

~*~

"I have four offers on the land. One is for all of it, the other is...hang on. That line is ringing again." She'd meant to give him the good news, but it was too busy to do right now. "I'll have to call you back, Kinsey. The offers are coming in very fast now. I suspect by the end of the day, you'll have sold the land, making it so you don't have to farm anymore. I'll call you back here in a bit."

Hanging up on Kinsey, she picked up the other line. It was her old friend, Winchester. He wanted to know when the bidding stopped. Stupid question. It would go on until it was finished, and one man was left. She told him that, but in a much nicer way. The man laughed like he knew she was being nice in the way she told him.

"How much is the bid for now?" She said that she was still answering the phone, so she'd have to look. "Well, get on it, girl. My land is wasting away right now. And you know that I get what I want. I should have had you tell them others that so they'd back off. But I want this land, and I'm going to have to spend some of my hard-earned cash to get it, I'm thinking. Making this Pennington man a very wealthy person."

"You might not win this time, you know. There are some pretty heavy hitters bidding on this land, and

I'm only going to have to deal with one of you." He doubled his last bid and told her to let him know when she knew anything. "You know I will. I was actually thinking of having conference calls set up in the office so that I could hear them all at once."

"Excellent idea. I'll be there in an hour." Before she could tell him that she was joking, he hung up on her. The only other person she wanted here was Kinsey, and she didn't think it would be a good idea to have him here fainting when he heard how much the price was up to now. She had her secretary call the other three men and tell them what was going on. They all agreed to come to the meeting room and bid on the land in person. Kinsey was going to shit his pants when he heard the amount that was being tossed around for the land that he wanted rid of.

When the other three men arrived, they sat in the conference room and talked before she came in and told them the last bid on the land. None of them seemed inclined to bid, but she knew better; they all wanted the land and were determined to get it. As she was leaving them to it, David caught her hand.

"You think you can round us up some whiskey and some food, darling? I'd like to get drunk and claim myself as a winner, but I have to get these other men a good showing." She said that she'd see what she could do for him. "Don't go cheap on us now, darling. We're going to be making you have a bit of pocket money too. My momma would say that to me. She'd say, Davey, honey, I need a bit of pocket money, and I'd give her the world if she wanted it. God rest her old soul. You fix us up a bit here."

Calling back Kinsey, she was glad that he put her on speaker phone for the details, as his brothers were all there, including Raphael. She was catching their excitement even over the phone. She not only told them what the bidding was up to, but how the men were in her conference room right now, having the time of their lives trying to outdo one another.

"They're the biggest dealers in land that I've ever worked with." Gleason asked her what that meant. "They have the most money. And by that I mean that they're all billionaires, all of them."

"So you have four billionaires in your office right now having a bidding war on our land. You said it's over the asking price, is that normal?" She told Bodi that it was when there was this much land at stake. "How much longer do you suppose they'll work this over? I mean, will they be in there for days?"

"No, I'm predicting that by the end of work today, they'll have hashed it all out and one will be considered the winner. I'm betting on Winchester, but I don't know for sure. He's a big hitter and is known for having vast land deals in his favor." Kinsey asked if she'd call them back. "Of course I will. As soon as I know, you'll know too. How late can I call you guys? I know that you go to bed early."

"Anytime." They said that in unison, and it made her laugh a little. "Just when you have news, no matter the time, you call us. We'll not sleep anyway, waiting for this to be finished. At least I know that I'm not going to be sleeping anytime soon."

As soon as she hung up with the brothers, she called Kinsey back. He told her that he had a call from someone named Winchester this morning and that he'd left a message about getting together with him about the land. Kinsey asked her if that was normal and how he got his name and number.

"The land has for sale signs all over the place; it wouldn't take much for a person with money to be able to hunt you down. As for getting the number, it wouldn't be that difficult either. What did he say about the deal?" Kinsey told her. "So he's thinking he's going to win, and decided you could tell him more about the place than anyone else can. I guess I can see that. He's a nice enough person, but wealthy. It's up to you if you want to call him back, but I'd wait to see who wins. It's sort of fun to listen to them tossing around money like they are. You'd have a heart attack. But I'd be there for you."

"I nearly did when you said they were

billionaires. I've never met one before. I mean, I know that they're out there, I just never had the occasion to meet any one of them." She laughed, then told him that he had. "Are you telling me that you're a billionaire?" His voice told her that he didn't believe that she was one, too.

"I am because I own this company. We've been in business for a good long time and have long-reaching arms when it comes to money. My grannie made this company shine when she was in charge of it, and now I'm doing even better. As I said, we're an old company and people trust us with their money and businesses." He didn't say anything. "Kinsey, it's all right. It's just money."

"Says the person who just told me that they're a billionaire." This time, his voice sounded hard, like he was mad at her or something. "I didn't know when I started out seeing you." She asked him if it would have made a difference. "Of course it does. You're rich and I'm barely making ends meet here."

"We'll be in the same boat after this sale, though I don't know why it should matter. You'll have money too. Do you think I've treated you differently because I have money and you don't?" He said that she'd not, but that didn't mean anything. "It means everything. Especially if you have any thoughts not seeing me anymore because of a few bucks."

"It's not a few bucks, though, is it? I mean, we're talking a lot of money here." She asked him when he became a snob. "I'm not a snob, but you told me that you sometimes need someone to take you to dinners, and would you want me at your side?"

"Yes." She said that without hesitation to him. "Would you do the same for me? Would you want to date me only if I have no money? I've enjoyed our time together, meeting at your house and out to dinner at times. Grannie likes you, too."

"I don't know how I'd feel taking you out to dinner at what I could afford before this." Instead of talking to him more, she told him she'd call him when she had a number and hung up. Her heart was broken, and she wasn't sure why. Could she have fallen in love with the man in such a short time? Her broken heart certainly felt like it.

Making herself be busy, she ignored the pain in her chest and decided that she was just hurt by his words. It couldn't be that she was in love with the big idiot and now that he'd shown his true colors she — he'd shown his not the other way around — she was going to move on with her life and do what all people did that had been dumped by the man of their dreams. They moved on, she kept telling herself.

It was nearly quitting time when she heard from the group of men. Putting on the best smile that she could, she asked them who had won. It was all she could do not to sob when they told her not only the amount of money that was the winning bid, but who had won it. It had been as she thought all along. It had been David Winchester. He'd now be considered the richest man in the country and the richest landowner in the country as well. Now all she had to do was call the Pennington family — not Kinsey alone but just the family, and let them know that they were wealthy men, all of them.

Dialing the number that was as much a part of her memory as the man to whom it belonged to, she made herself smile and put on a happy face. Once he answered, she told him how much the winning bid was, plus she'd have the checks for him in five days. There was still a lot of paperwork that needed to be processed before anyone could claim anything.

After giving him the information, Meggie hung up the phone and sat at her desk, sobbing. He'd broken her heart, and the only way that he could have done that was for her to have fallen in love with the big ox.

Chapter 6

Kinsey kept himself busy by doing all the work that came with owning the farm. Mr. Winchester had said that he'd take care of the cattle that were on the farm. He said for them to just pack up what they wanted and that he'd take care of the rest. Kinsey supposed he didn't want them to mess up the sale in any way by taking things that no longer belonged to them. The man was even coming to the house tomorrow night for a *look-see* to see what his money had bought him.

"What the hell is wrong with you?" He looked at Wylie and asked him what he meant. "You're tossing that cow around like she owes you money, and you're going to get it. So again, what the fucking hell is wrong with you?"

"I don't know what you're talking about." But he did. Gleason had caught him doing the same thing yesterday. Backing away from the cow, he put his hands up like he'd been arrested. His head was killing him, and there was just too much going on for him not to be just a little upset. "I've got a lot on my mind."

"Meggie." He turned to look around so fast,

thinking that she was here, that he nearly unmaned himself with the rope he had on his belt. He looked at his brother. "I see. Well, I don't, but I have a clue. You're not seeing her anymore. Was she only dating you so she could make some money off the sale?"

"Only you would blame her." He turned back to his job. "I don't know what you're talking about. We had a good time, and now it's over. It was good while it lasted, but she's got money, and well, she's got lots of money."

"Hey, moron. So do you." He glanced at Gleason and told him that they didn't have it yet. Red tape had caused things to be delayed from Mr. Winchester. Something about the land deals that were out of the state. "You broke it off with her on account of her having a bit more money than we do? I got it right then, you are a moron. I thought you guys had something special."

"We didn't." Liar, he called himself. Something that he'd been doing since he'd spoken to her a week and a half ago. He was a liar who was lying to himself daily about them not having anything special, too. It was love. He had stupidly fallen in love with a woman who could have bought them out with one signature on a checkbook. "Just leave it alone, Gleason. I'm not in the mood to go over shit that isn't any of your business."

"Well, I guess I learned something today. How not to treat a woman from my big brother 'the moron' when it comes to women." Gleason didn't speak about it anymore. As the saying went on, he realized that he wasn't speaking to him at all. Just as well, the conversation in his head was driving him crazy enough with the way he was browbeating himself.

By the time the milk was loaded and gone, he was ready to call it a day. Just yesterday, he quit carrying his cell phone around, so he wasn't forever looking to see if Meggie had called him back. He didn't know what he'd say to her, but he did want to hear her voice again. Even though the last time she'd been pretty upset with him when he'd told her that he couldn't go on a date with her to her conference next week. So she asked Wylie to take her.

He'd tried his best not to be upset with his brother. He'd guessed that they had fought over the dating thing, but he was still taking her. She'd told Wylie that she didn't want to be hit on, and a big man would help. Wylie was a big man and smart, too. He'd told him that he wasn't going to take her if it bothered him that much.

"I don't mind." He wanted to tell him that he did indeed mind, but didn't. What good would it do him to make a claim on a rich woman. "You go ahead and protect her from other men like me. Only the ones that want to get into her pants."

"I don't believe at all that that's what it was like between the two of you. I'd say you're about halfway into loving her." He didn't even look at him. "Kinsey, tell me if this is going to bother you, and I'll not go. As it is now, she's only out the cost of a tux that she rented for me."

"Aren't your clothes good enough?" As soon as the words were out of his mouth, he knew he'd made a mistake. His brother only looked at him like he knew that he'd pushed the right buttons. "I'm just kidding around. Of course, you'd have to dress up. I bet she's going to be dressed to the nines too. All dolled up too."

"You should be doing this." He just turned his back on Wylie and told him that the better man was taking her. "Well, you do have that right. You'd probably use the wrong fork or something."

He would never know just how much that hurt him if he'd not been thinking the same thing for the past few days. Everything that he did reminded him of how much better she was than him, that she'd grown up with money, and he was only just now getting a bit. A lot of a bit, but he'd not had the manners that she'd need pounded into his head growing up. There were vast differences between the two of them, and the sooner she thought of them, the better off...he didn't think he was ever going to be better off knowing that he was nothing compared to her. When he got into the house to finish up supper, there were three messages on his phone. It was David Winchester.

"I'm invited to this conference as the lead speaker tomorrow night. Now that you've got some money, I expect you to be my plus-one on the invite. My wife can't go, some other commitment — family stuff that I didn't know about, or I wouldn't have okayed this here thing. But I'm not taking no for an answer. I like you and I'm wanting you to go with me. I'll have a car there by five-thirty tomorrow night, and you'll be ready."

There were two other messages with the same thing on them. More about the family stuff that he wished he was going to, but each one of them had said he wasn't taking no for an answer. He didn't feel like he could say no; the man had spent his hard-earned money on buying him out, so he had to go. He had no idea what he was going to do about seeing Meggie there.

Kinsey decided to call Wylie and tell him about the invite. They might not even be the same conference. He was sure that rich people had them all the time. As the phone rang, he decided that he should warn Meggie, too, that he was going to be there. He didn't think she'd make a scene, but he didn't know her all that well in knowing if she'd do that or not.

"Kinsey, have you ever been fitted for a tux?" He

said that he'd not, and asked him what the difference was between just pulling them off the rack. "Let me tell you, it's kind of personal. They measure you. I mean, they measure all of you." His laughter had him laughing. "What can I do for you?"

"I'm going to the conference with Winchester." He thought that he should have worked up to it, but knowing Wylie like he did, he'd more than likely find something else to be long-winded about. "He made it sound like I had to go, and if I didn't, he'd be disappointed in me or something. I don't want to go. I guess I'll have to be measured too. Where are you?"

"In Columbus. I'll give you directions in a minute. Is this going to cause trouble, Kin? I mean, you turned down Meggie. What's she going to think when you tell her?" He said that he'd say the same thing that Winchester had given him no out. "I don't know if you believe that or not, but you showing up is going to be different. Don't you think? I mean, I'm with the seller, you with the buyer. What will people think?"

"What people think is whatever they're going to think, I guess." He wished he'd said that to Meggie the other day. "I wondered if you could call her and give her—"

"Nope. I'm nope-ing right out of that. You call her. This is on you." He pleaded with him. "Not going to happen. And you'd better be getting your ass here to be measured, too. The thing is tomorrow night."

"All right. Give me the directions. I wish you'd call her for me." He told him again that he wasn't going to do that. "I'll be there in an hour. Can they fit me in?"

After being assured that Mr. Winchester had called to have him pushed into the time, he was set to go. After some advice from Wylie about being measured, he took a quick shower to get the cow off him and headed in. Calling Meggie while he drove was a big no-no, but he had to tell her now or she'd never get her told.

He tried her office first and was told that she'd gone home for the day. After dialing her cell phone, he pulled up in front of the bank to get some cash. He didn't know how much was in the account, but he'd need some money to pay for the tux. He didn't figure that Winchester was paying for his too. Getting what he could out of the account, more than he'd need surely, he was on his way and talking to Meggie.

"I'm an idiot." He had no idea where that had come from and pulled off the side of the road so that he could tell her what else he'd been. "I would ask you to forgive me, but I'm sure you've written me off for some kind of loon."

"Kinsey, I'd never do that. Let me put you on hold. I have David on the other line. He's telling me that his plus-one tomorrow night is you." So much for it being a different conference. While he listened to music playing, he pulled back into traffic. Hoping that the truck would make it that far, he spoke to the vehicle like he always did.

"Come on, baby, you know you want to go to Columbus. I just gave you that wax job last night for Wylie to use you to go to town. Remember that?" Patting the dashboard, he smiled at the shifter. "We've come a long way, you and I, and you have to remember who wanted to keep you when no one else did."

"Are you talking to your truck?" He was embarrassed and could feel his face heating up. "I don't think you ever talked to me that way. Did you?"

"No. I didn't need to. You were the best thing that I could have had." She cleared her throat and told him to behave himself. She had things to do today. "So do I. I have to go be fitted for a tux. I was hoping that it was a different conference, but I'm guessing that I'd be wrong about that, too."

"Would you like for it to be different? I mean, I have to go, so does David, but you and Wylie are going to keep us out of trouble. David usually gets out of these things, but this time he's going, and he said it's to introduce you to the people you'll be hanging out with." He asked her what that meant. "Rich people. I take it you have no idea what this conference is about?"

"No. I mean, if you told me I don't remember.

And Winchester only said I was going and nothing more. What kind of thing is this?" She told him. Kinsey nearly rear-ended a car, he'd been so preoccupied with what she'd said to him. "What's that mean, a get-together for the new rich and old money? Do people still care if you're new money or old?"

"You did." He had and felt like a shit because he'd taken it out on her. "You can't back out on David. He's hoping you keep him from drinking too much and buying shit that he doesn't need. And there will be a lot of people at this thing with bright new ideas to sell to anyone who is stupid with their money. We're both sure that you'll be able to do that. At least David is."

"You think I'd be stupid with my money?" She said that he'd not spend a dime of it unless it came with all kinds of guarantees and backup plans. "I feel like that's a dig to me, but you're more than likely right. I'll more than likely have the same money that I started with in ten years."

"I hope not." She laughed and she told him she was sorry. "I've not had a great deal to laugh about over the last few days. By the way, all your money will be transferred to the accounts that were given to me by noon today. It's been cleared for you to spend as much as you'd like. All six of you."

"I think that Gleason has a house that he's been

eyeing. It's not right in town, but outside of it. I was surprised when he went too big." She told him she thought Gleason would make all his money work for him. "And I won't?" She didn't say anything, and he told her not to answer that.

"As you said, you'll have the same money in a few years, and none of you will wonder at all what you spent your money on. You'll know exactly what it is you've bought and will be proud of it." He told her that he'd be proud of anything he purchased. "I know you will." She didn't say anything for several minutes, and he had to look at the phone to make sure she hadn't hung up on him.

"I just wanted to warn you that I'd be there too. I wish I had known what it's about, but I guess people would find out sooner or later. I miss you, Meggie." She sounded like she was crying, and when she blew her nose, he knew it. "I'm so sorry that I was a fool. I miss talking to you every day. And working with you. I don't know anything about what you do for a living, but I'm sure it's something very important."

"I'm only important to people with money who need to spend. Oh, Kinsey, I miss you too. Everything about you is all I can think about. I want to start over." He said that he wanted to pick up where they left off if she'd let him. "I'll let you do anything that puts you back in my life. I've fallen in love with you, and I can't stand my life without you around."

"You love me?" She said that she thinks she has from the moment that he first called her. "I love you, too, honey. I wish I didn't have to go to this thing tomorrow night, but we'll talk later. Mr. Winchester is coming over the following night to talk to us about what we're leaving. Did you know that he is going to tear down the house and put a bigger one in? He said that he's going to live on the property that has come to mean so much to him."

He got out of the truck, so happy that it made it all the way there, and went into the tailor's shop. He'd never had anything tailored in his life, and now he was getting a tux. He wondered if he'd be able to use his brand new credit card he'd gotten to go with his brand new status as a rich man. Words that he never thought he'd ever say about himself.

"I have a busy schedule here that I have to get finished before I can leave early." He told her what he was doing. "Don't forget to buy two suits, too, Kinsey. I have three more business meetings that I have to go to, and you're going to be on my arm when I go."

She hung up before he could say anything. Wylie was still there, and he told him that he'd made up with Meggie. Of course, he had to go on about how he knew that they'd had a fight and that they were in love. It occurred to him that he'd not told her that he loved her, too, at least he couldn't remember telling her, but he was going to tell her every minute of every day from now on.

Being introduced to the tailor, Mr. Wayneright told him that he did all of Mr. Winchester's suits and tuxedos. After telling him that he would need to be measured for two suits, it didn't seem to bother the man, but he did tell him that they'd have to do two different measurements then. He was shocked that he'd not even considered the price of them. His way of thinking was that having two of them would go a long way in all kinds of settings. He was being measured when he thought of something else.

He was going to have to get him a new truck. Or a car. Whatever rich men drove around. But he'd keep the old one too for work around...he didn't have a place to work and was going to have to take care of that soon too. He needed to work. After that, all he did was empty out his head with his brother. Wylie could make him laugh when no one else could.

~*~

Meggie decided at the last minute to wear the black dress instead of the blue one. They weren't all that different; both of them were expensive gowns, but the black one showed off more of her body than the blue one did. And tonight she wanted to be as sexy as hell for the man that she loved. Her grannie noticed the difference in her as soon as she came in the door at a little after two in the afternoon.

"Well, well, well. Someone has fallen in love again. Who could be the lucky man?" She told her that Kinsey had told her he was sorry. "I knew that he would. He just can't live without my little girl. Have you told him that you love him too?"

"I did. And he told me that he loves me too. Oh, Grannie, what am I going to do all evening with another man on my arm?" Grannie told her. "I'm not going to make him jealous. I have enough on my hands with keeping him happy that he's wealthy. I don't know how long this will last, but I'm going to make it last for as long as I can."

Getting ready was fun. She'd not wanted to go, but this conference helped a great many people with new ideas and sparked growth and economy all over the country. Once she was dressed, she took her time with her makeup, knowing that this one time she was going to be everything she could be. Laughing, she was putting on her shoes when her grannie came to her room.

"Now, don't freak out." She told her that everyone did when someone said that to them. "I know, but this one is important for you not to freak out. There's been an accident."

"Who?" She put her shoes down, wondering

why her heart was suddenly beating loud enough to be heard by her. "Was anyone killed? You know, when you start with there has been an accident, you should also say whether or not anyone was killed."

"No one was killed. Though you might think so when I tell you what happened. The police said that if he'd been in a newer car, he would have been killed, but lucky for him, he was driving his grandda's truck." So it had to be Kinsey. Nodding, she stood up to get something more suitable on than what she had been going to wear to the conference. "What are you doing?"

"I'm changing to go to the hospital. I'm also assuming that it's Kinsey. Right?" Grannie nodded, and all the air in her body just exploded out of her. She had to sit down. "You said he wasn't killed. That's wonderful news, but I have a feeling that there's more to it than that. Just tell me."

"He was sitting in stopped traffic when a semi rolled up behind him and rear-ended him. He was shoved up under the semi in front of him. Luckily, for as old as the vehicle was, all it did was bend metal and not break plastic. He's gone to the hospital for the cuts on his face and hands." She stood up to change again. "I told him I'd make you go to the conference. But I also made him understand that you were younger than me and thus better at telling me to go screw myself than I was. He's going to be all right. A concussion for sure, but there aren't any broken bones, Wylie told me."

"Is Wylie going to the hospital with his brother? And have you called any of the others?" She said that she'd not thought of the others. And yes, he was going with his brother, so was David. "I'll call them to make sure that they understand that he's going to be all right. Also, tell them to drive carefully. Or better yet, don't drive at all. I'm not going to drive."

"Are you going to the conference?" The black silk slipped off her shoulders and onto the carpet as she was stepping into her closet. "I guess that's a big no, too. He's going to be upset with you if you don't go."

"I'll make him understand that rich people like poor people want to make sure that the man they love is going to be all right when I see him. Or something along those lines." She came out of her closet with a pair of jeans and a T-shirt on. "Did you really talk to him?"

"I didn't. I could hear him talking calmly to Wylie, who wasn't calm by the way, but he's going to think that I screwed this up by not telling you that you had to go to the thing tonight." She told her grannie he'd get over it. "I'm sure that he will. Also, you should know that he saved Wylie from being hurt. When he realized what was going on, he shoved Wylie down on the seat so he wasn't cut at all. David was in the limo behind the semi and none the wiser about what happened to his date tonight. I'm starting to feel the effects of this accident now. Oh lordy, he could have been killed. Both of them might well have been—"

"Don't talk like that. We know that they're both fine, and we're going to concentrate on that. Are you going with me?" She asked if she was really not driving. "I'm not. I don't think that I could right now. We'll get Roger to drive us. I knew I was going to regret not having a driver on staff. See what I do when I'm depressed? From now on, I don't make decisions when I'm down in the dumps."

"Meggie, you're babbling." She said she knew that and wasn't going to stop until she could see Kinsey. "All right. I'll go too. The boy was starting to grow on me, and I'd like to make sure that he's all right, too. So long as you're sure you're not driving. You know how Roger can be. He's slower than I am when it comes to driving."

"He'll be fine. We'll get there in one piece and we'll be fine for it." She looked at her grannie as she tied her tennis shoes. "He's really all right, isn't he? I don't want to go there and find out that he passed away after we just made up."

"He's fine, honey. Get your phone. I have a feeling that you're going to need it." They were out the door in twenty minutes. Roger did drive the speed limit, but he got them there on time, and that was all that mattered to her. Now to find Kinsey and Wylie.

She'd called the brothers and told them what was going on while riding to the hospital. Raphael was home today and was going to come in with the others. Since Kinsey was at a larger hospital, they didn't need to have instructions on how to find it. She loved these men too and would tell them when she saw them. It was Gleason who asked several times if their brother was all right, but she found that she didn't care. Saying it to him made her feel like he really was all right and that he was going to be fine, too.

Meggie was having a hard time getting any information from the people at the hospital. She wasn't his wife, so they'd not tell her much more than he was there and being looked at. It wasn't until the other four showed up that she was shown not just where he was but allowed to be with him while the doctor spoke to him after he was examined. Which was taking a good deal longer than she thought it should have. The doctor told her that he really was fine, but cut up pretty badly.

"I'm going to keep the two of them overnight. That way, we can make sure that they're not going to have any trouble with concussions tonight. Wylie Pennington isn't hurt as badly, but he did hit his head on the dashboard when the truck was totaled. Kinsey Pennington sustained more injuries due to his being upright when the truck was pushed up under the semi in front of him. Mr. Winchester has also made it very clear that you're all going to be staying the night to keep an eye on the gentlemen." The doctor smiled a little. "We've known Mr. Winchester for some time now, and what he wants, he gets. We know better than to do anything differently. He's a good donor for this university and the hospitals."

Kinsey was getting his head examined, and she'd still not gotten to see him as yet. When Wylie said her name, she went right to him and held his hand. Wherever his brother was, he'd better be getting as good care as they said, or she was going to know the reason why. Telling him that she had him, Wylie sobbed like he'd been hurt worse than she'd been told, and it worried her.

"You should have seen him, honey. Barking out orders like he was in the service. I don't know why I thought that he'd be hysterical, but there he was, calm as one of the cows after milking them." She laughed and he did too. "He's just fine, Meggie. I saw him. I know you guys have to see him, too, but I promise you that he's just fine. We're both going to be sore tomorrow, but we're alive and that's all that matters, don't you think?"

"I do, Wylie. I really do think that's all that matters." She put her forehead to his. "If you didn't want to be my date tonight, there are lots of better ways to get out of it instead of having an accident."

"You were all he talked about while we were waiting on the police to come. Me shoved up under the dash, and him holding me there. He kept telling me that he had me, and it calmed me down that he did." A nurse came in and told him he was going to go to X-ray. "I just need to tell you one more thing. He loves you. When we were at the tailors, he told me that he didn't remember if he told you or not. I told him that was a pretty important thing to forget about, and he assured me that he was going to do it daily from now on. I hope he marries you, Meggie. It'll be the greatest love story to tell our kids someday."

While he was gone, she saw David. The man was driving everyone crazy, making sure that they had everything they needed. After being introduced to the other men, she told him to sit down and shut up. She couldn't believe it when he did. Especially after his wife showed up. They were alike, the two of them, barking orders to get everyone taken care of. She'd never realized how old the man looked until right then. He was old enough, she thought, to be the men's father and wondered if he felt that way toward Kinsey. It would make sense, she thought. He was making sure that they were all taken care of, including herself and her Grannie.

Meggie thought that she might be a little bit in love with David too, in a father sort of way, and smiled when he asked her for the fourth time if she was all right. Then Kinsey was wheeled in, and there was no one else but him. But she did find herself waiting until his brothers got to see him. Sobbing when she was finally able to touch him, she told him several times that she loved him and was glad that he didn't have any issues with telling her the same thing. She was only as strong as the man who was holding her, and that was pretty good, she thought.

Chapter 7

Walton read about the accident in the newspaper. He'd been reading an article about the prison system being too kind to prisoners when the headlines said there had been a trucking accident that nearly took the lives of four people. Then, after reading it, he didn't understand the four people any better than anyone else would have. As his family was just fine.

"Fine enough to come see me once in a while, you'd think." He didn't care that people stared at him for talking to himself. He was here for life without parole. They needed to be doing what he said and not the other way around. "I ain't seen hide nor hair of them since I've been in here. You'd think that I didn't mean anything to them."

He knew that he more than likely didn't mean shit to them. He'd killed off their mother, and that's all that they saw about him. Durn near twelve years now in here and not one of them had even written him a letter or sent him any birthday money.

"Ingrates. All of them." He had to think how old the oldest one was now. The youngest, he was still in school when he'd killed Martha. However, he didn't know their names anymore other than ingrates, but that was fine by him. He'd get out of here one day, and they'd be sorry for leaving him behind like he didn't mean shit to them. "Ingrates. Damned shits are all they are."

Martha hadn't even been good to him when she'd been alive. She'd never wanted to marry him in the first place. Bitching about this or that, and how the farm was making her sick. And how there wasn't enough money to go around to feed them all. He was just unlucky at cards, that was all. And he killed her because she told him she was leaving him on the farm on his own. Well, that's what he told people. She wanted him to leave the farming to her and the ingrates, and he just didn't cotton to that.

"I'd showed her being sick, didn't I?" Sometimes the words up in his head made more sense than they did when he spilled them out. "Stupid bitch just had to beg me to kill her, didn't she? Couldn't leave well enough alone. Not her. The stupid cow. She had to have the last word in—"

"You've been told about that, Pennington. Keep your trap shut if you aren't talking to someone directly. You make the other inmates afraid of you." He said that he didn't mean no harm. One thing that he knew, you didn't piss off the ones with the guns, no sir. "See that you keep your mouth shut too when it's dinnertime. I'm sick of you making it so people have to crowd into one table because you're acting like you're off your meds again."

"I'm not on any meds. You know it too." He just walked away with his hand on his gun. Stupid screws were forever trying to piss him off. "I'll be quiet when I want to, too. You'll see. I ain't got nothing to do with them crowding into one table either."

He, of course, said that barely under his breath so that he'd not be in trouble again. They put him in solitary confinement when he acted out. While he didn't like people, he hated his own company even more.

Looking at the article again, he wondered if any of them were married yet and taking after him. He hoped so. His greatest pleasure would be introducing his kids around to the others in here. It was a big deal to some of these people when a son or two followed in your footsteps and ended up in the big house.

Walton thought that he'd like that. To have some of his kids following in his footsteps. Be just like the old man. His momma would have had a fit, though, and she was the one who held the purse strings all the time. He wondered what had happened to her and decided that she must have died some time ago.

"She was already old when I came out of her."

He looked around to see if any of the guards were close to him and decided that they were giving him the eye, and he went back to his cell. There wasn't anything in there to occupy his mind, so he took the paper with him. He still wanted to read that article about the prison system being too soft on their prisoners. "Like hell they are."

Walton had been in prison more than he'd been out. This here last time had put him in for good, and there wasn't any way he was getting out. He liked to talk big about it, saying that he was going to have that overturned, but in the years he'd been in here, nobody ever told him that he had a parole hearing or nothing.

When he was just fourteen, he was put into the system. His momma told him he could rot in there; she wasn't going to get him out. So he spent the next four years of his life in and out of juvey homes until he got to go to the big house. It was his eighteenth birthday when he was caught stealing his momma's car. And damned if she didn't call the police on him before he was out of the driveway. He got arrested and spent the next week waiting for someone to come and bail him out. It was then that he met Martha.

She'd been a bit older than him and had herself a real job. Working for the city, she would go into the jails and clean them up. He wooed her as much as one can for a stupid kid, and she kept right on coming around when he was sentenced to six months of highway duty out on Route 40. Easiest job he'd ever had in his life.

After getting her knocked up the first time, he had to marry her. Her daddy held a gun right to his head when they were saying their vows at the justice of the peace. No peace about it. She sobbed the entire time, telling her daddy that she wanted nothing to do with him and that he'd just beat her if she were his wife. Of course, he did that, and her dad never said a word. Said they was married now and she'd have to put up with whatever he gave her.

She had him a little boy the first time, and he felt like he was king of the hill that first night. Right up until he got caught robbing the convenience store down the road from where they were living. Nobody believed him when he said it was for diapers. He had nearly forty dollars on himself that didn't belong to the store.

Martha still worked for the city cleaning jail cells. About the only time he got to see her was when she was cleaning the cells he was in. But that didn't stop her from popping out one boy after another. He had him a good half dozen of them, and he thought that his momma would be so proud of him. All she did was scream at him for losing more farm land to cards.

"She hit me a bunch, too." She didn't, but he liked to tell people that was why he sold off the farm.

He was forever looking for the next big win at cards, and it never came. But he lost a lot of land that way, and it pissed his momma off so much that she went and took his name off the land and put it in her own. "Damned women ain't got no sense at all if you asked me. How was I supposed to get more money if it ain't coming to me? I suppose she gave it over to the boys, too. Like that's the right thing to do."

His momma had come to see him one time. Right after the youngest, he thought his name was Eric or something like that. He never knew any of their names after he was told what it was. Just numbered them one through six. That worked until it didn't no more, and they all looked to be about the same height. But she'd had plenty to say to him then.

"Them boys are going to do all right by me." He asked her then why they didn't do right by him, sending him a little money now and again. "Because they aren't as stupid as you are, thank the good lord. You listen to me now. They went and joined up as soon as they was out of school so they could get them a free education."

"Joined up to what? I'm not going to like it if you tell me that they joined some gang or something. That's no way to make any money, don't you know." She just stared at him, and he told her he would shut up now. "They is my boys, you understand?"

"Thankfully, they're nothing like you. But they joined the Army, all six of them did. The last one is going to come out in three years. Anyway, they got all but a hundred acres back of the family land. I hope they sell it all and spend the money on something sustainable. Like a house and a new car. Kinsey is still driving that truck of your father's." He had to ask her who that was. "Your oldest son, you idiot. I swear to Christ, you get stupider every time I try to have a conversation with you. Do you understand what it is I'm telling you? I'm not leaving the farm to you, but that oldest of yours. So he'll take care of his brothers."

"Again, why ain't they taking care of me?" She did that eye thing where he would swear that she was looking right into his brain and knowing his every thought. "I was just asking. A man has a right to expect his kids to take care of him in his golden years."

"You ain't never going to have a golden time until you're dead. And they ain't gonna take care of you if I have anything to say about it. You're useless and they know it. Killed their momma like she was nothing at all. Why'd you have to go and do something like that? They loved her."

"Well, I didn't." He hadn't either, and that made his momma sore at him again. But she had gone on about how he was getting nothing from her, and she told them boys of his daily that they needed to sell out and get a life. "How much you figuring it'll be worth? I couldn't get anyone to bid on any of the land since you took it out of my name. Damn, but that was mean of you."

"Good." She told him about a bunch of stuff that was going to happen when she passed on and how he wasn't going to be mentioned in her will. After hearing that, he just tuned her out until her time was up and she could get away from him. "I won't be back, and as surely as I'm standing here, I'm not going to tell those boys to come and visit you either. You don't deserve them even though they're only here because of a bit of spit that came out of that peter of yours."

After she left, he had to wonder if something she said to him was important. And in all the years since then, nothing had ever come to bite him in the ass. Putting the paper in the trash can, he just knew that they were clamoring to get to see him, and he'd have to make sure that they did right by him.

"A little money in my pot won't go unnoticed either." But in order to get that, he'd have to know who to call, and since he didn't even know their names at all, he was pretty sure that he wasn't going to be visited by them any too soon either. "That's funny how that worked."

Remembering that one of them had been named in the paper, he had to read the article three more times until he found two names. Wylie, like the coyote in them old time cartoons that he used to watch as a kid, and Kinsey. It sounded like a girl's name to him.

It took him nearly three hours to get someone to help him. Once they were set up to find the names of his two boys all he had to do was sit back and wait. Maybe there would be some money coming in from the accident. He'd be getting some of that or know the reason why. They told him that he could have the phone numbers on Thursday, when it was his turn to use the phones.

"Damned people outta know that my kids are special to me. They'd been in an accident, haven't they?" He was told to shut up again and did so. There was some money riding on getting to talk to them, and he wasn't going to screw that up. When he realized it was Friday and not Monday like he thought, he didn't know if he could be good for a whole week. He'd have to be extra careful about the guards not taking the numbers back from him.

Walton had trouble being good from hour to hour, much less days. It was the talking to himself that got him into the most trouble. He could have hours of conversations that turned out that he was smarter than he thought before someone would take exception to him talking all the time. People just didn't understand him and they was jealous of him being able to be in here and not go stark raving mad. He kind of liked the quietness of the days and the way everything was the same.

He figured that if he stayed in his cell, he'd not cause so much trouble. He could talk to himself there and get the answers that he wanted before anyone noticed. The guards would come by and check on him once in a while, and that was fine by him. He usually got in a question or two before they just simply moved on. He was like that, questioning everything.

As he was closing his eyes that night, he thought of the next five or six days. He was going to be plum worn out when Thursday rolled around again, but it would be worth it to see what his children were up to and, more importantly, to tell them they needed to bring him some money.

~*~

Kinsey held her hand as best he could. He had sprained his wrist holding down his brother, and it was painful for the most part. When they said that they were going to X-ray it again, he decided that he needed something for pain. It was beginning to hurt a great deal then.

Having Meggie at his side helped with so many things. The thoughts of the accident played in his mind, and all he could see was that he'd been lucky that he'd not been cut in half. That and the fact that Wylie had been all right and not killed either had made him feel like he was going to be sick when he thought about how bad it could have been. Then he'd gotten a look at his grandpa's old truck.

It was crushed like an accordion. The front end was close to the seats they'd been sitting in, and the bed of it looked like one of those short truck beds he'd seen in drawings. It was the way that the hood of the truck had been crushed down about ten inches that made him think that it could have been him and his brother under the semi in front of them.

"Do you know how many stitches you have in your head?" He told Gleason that he didn't know and had asked not to be told. The outcome was better than it should have been, he thought. "That's for sure. When I saw the truck, all I could think about was that there wasn't enough room in it for one person, much less the two of you."

"I don't want to think about it." They said they understood and changed the subject. David came in then and was much calmer than he'd been when he'd seen him at the accident site. He'd been telling people that they were to be careful with his family, which had the police believing that he was their father. No one seemed to be able to get him to stop, either. Which, to Kinsey, had been all right. He was getting things done, and he was starting to feel the effects of the accident even then. He asked David about the conference.

"It'll go on without us. Just a shame I couldn't take you there. It would have been fun for the two of us." He said that he'd go next year. "Yes, but you'll take a limo then. I don't want to come up on a scene like that again. I nearly had myself a heart attack seeing the two of you all bunched up in that metal mess. Like the officer told you, it was lucky that you were driving that old thing, or you might well have been killed." David shivered. "No, that's not a sight that I'm going to easily not think of when I see the two of you again."

When he was taken down to X-ray, he was nearly sobbing for something for the pain. If this was what a sprained wrist felt like, he never would make fun of his brothers again when they turned their ankles. It had happened a few times on the farm, and he was going to be more sympathetic toward them from now on. By the time he was back in his room, he was nearly cross-eyed with pain.

"It's broken." It didn't make it feel any better to know that, but he was glad for the pain medications now that he could have them. "We missed it the first time with all the other things going on. We'll have to prep you for surgery now and get it taken care of."

Closing his eyes, he would have agreed to anything now because of the medication he'd been given. It was wonderful stuff, and he wanted to just sleep. Instead of him being allowed to rest even for a few minutes, he was told that he'd have to be ready to go down to the operating room to get the bones put back in place. He didn't care so long as they kept giving him whatever he had now.

Waking up, he forgot where he was. Not on that, but he didn't know what had happened for several minutes either. It was Bodi who told him he was all right and that the surgery had gone well. Falling asleep again, still no pain, he mumbled something about going home and decided that his brother was being nuts when he said that he wasn't going home anytime soon.

Whenever he woke, there was a different person in his room. Meggie was there each time, but his brothers or David would be switched out. Finally, when he thought that he needed to get things clear in his mind, he looked over at Meggie and smiled.

"You're so beautiful." She thanked him in a whisper. "Are we supposed to be quiet? I want to shout to the world that I'm in love with you." She told him that his brothers were sleeping and that he should allow them to do that. "But why are they here. I'm sure that the cows need to be milked."

"I've been having things taken care of at the farm. You just get better." David spoke to him from the other side of his bed, and it took him a few minutes to get his body to turn that way. "You've been through a great deal in the last twenty-four hours. Just let me take care of the farm now, and you take care of this little lady here. She's been here since you came in."

"She loves me." David laughed, and he seemed surprised by it. "Are you all right, David? You do look a little pale. You didn't get hurt, did you?"

"No, I'm fine now that I know you are." He thanked him. "No need for that. I was just glad that I was there. Calling the police was one of the hardest things—I've never had any trouble being calmed down before. Usually, I'm the one who makes all the decisions when there is an accident. I could be counted on to make sure that everyone was all right. But seeing you all smashed up in that truck…well, it's a sight that I never want repeated. The police said I did all right under the circumstances, but all I could do was stand there helplessly while you were hurting."

"I didn't hurt all that much. My wrist did, but not too bad. I kept thinking that Wylie needed me and I was going to be there for him." David nodded and wiped at the tears streaming down his cheeks. "I'm sorry, David. Please don't be upset. Everyone is fine. Wylie is just fine, and so am I."

"I know. I know that." He got up from his chair and moved toward the door. "You don't do that again, do you hear me? I don't know that—you've come to mean a great deal to me, Kinsey, you and your brothers.

I never had any children, but in the last couple of months, you've come to mean a great deal to me."

He left them then. Going out the door and to wherever he was headed. Meggie said that he'd end up in the cafeteria again and would be buying pie for anyone who wanted it. She'd said that he'd been doing that for the last few hours.

"I'd like some pie. But I guess he wants to buy it for strangers." She laughed a little and put her hand on his shoulder. "How are you doing? For the last several hours, all you've been doing is waking up, grunting a few times, and going back to sleep. Oh, before I forget, Ara is writing for the newspaper about the accident. He's making it an ongoing project so that people can keep up with your accident. Also, the prison called where your father is. He wants to get in touch with you for some reason. They said that they have your number from the accident."

Bodi moved over to sit with him, too. "They said that they'd give him the wrong number if you didn't want to speak to him. They don't care if he does one way or the other, but he'd seen the accident write-up in the paper and remembered that he had some kids. He only knows yours and Wylie's names from the article." He asked him how he was doing before continuing. "I don't care to talk to him, but it'll be up to you since you're the one that he's fixated on. I remember that from being a kid, how he'd get a new word or something that he'd learned told to him and he'd talk about it endlessly."

"He thinks there will be money from the accident." Bodi said that's what he figured, too. "Grandma said he'd remember us eventually. That he'd try his best to get us to come and see him or something like that. And that he'd want money. She also told us when we sell the farm, not to tell him or he'd be thinking that we should use it to try and get him out of prison too."

"She told me once he remembered us, we would have to be smart in not telling him anything good about us or he'd use it against us." Meggie asked him what that was supposed to mean. "Money. It all comes down to money to him. If he even thinks that we have some, he'll try his best to take it from us or, worse yet, to use it on one of his schemes. He was always trying to figure out a way to spend money. Especially when it was someone else's."

"Sounds like a great guy. I know that he killed your mother, but I don't think I ever heard how he'd done it. Was it so bad that it earned him no right to parole?"

"It was like his fifth strike against him. He did kill her in a horrific way, but since he'd been in and out of prison so much, they'd just put him there so he'd not hurt anyone else. Especially one of us for calling the police on him." Kinsey closed his eyes when he thought about how his momma had looked when their father had gotten done with her. "He'd beaten her nearly to death, and when he didn't kill her, he strangled her with her own belt. After that, he tried cutting her up with a chainsaw so that he could get rid of the evidence. He was making us help him. I don't think that Ara slept for a month without nightmares after that for a long time. Bodi, he won't to this day use a chainsaw without being sick."

"We were all there, but I think the younger two of us had it the hardest. We'd been with Momma all day that day, canning strawberry jam. The blood and the jam…it still haunts me to this day about the similarities of the two. I still can't make myself eat any strawberries or jam to this day." Meggie told him she was sorry she'd brought it up. "It's all right, honey. You have a right to know if you're going to be hanging around with us. But I won't go see him, Kinsey. Never. He can rot in there for all I care about him. I told you a long time ago that I'd only ever refer to him as Walton Pennington and nothing familial ever again."

"For that, I don't blame you. It would be hard for me to think of him as a father after doing that. And to bring you six in on it." She laid her head gently on his chest. "I wish I could have known your mother, or grannie for that matter, but I'm glad that I never got to know your father." She looked at him. "What are you going to do about him if he calls?"

"Nothing. I'm going to call the prison and tell them he can call if he wants, but it's not going to do him a bit of good. When he was around, he couldn't even remember our names, much less what order of birth we were." Kinsey laughed a little. "He called us by numbers for a long time, one through six. After we started getting taller than him, he'd sit down whenever he could so that it wouldn't look like he was smaller than any of us. And by smaller, I mean he was shorter and had no bulk at all. He was a short, skinny man without one brain cell in his head. I'll take care of him when he calls, if he calls. He'll get nothing from me about any of us either."

"I'd like to talk to the bastard." Raphael laughed as he stretched out in the chair. "He'd regret calling me, that's for sure. The man killed our momma when she'd done nothing wrong but tell him that he couldn't have a card party at the house as she'd been working all day making jam for the family."

Gleason and Wylie agreed that they didn't want to talk to him at all. It wasn't until the nurse came in to take his blood pressure that he decided he might as well get it over with on calling the prison. Once Meggie had the number for him, he didn't hesitate at all to call them and tell them that the only person he could call would be him. The others didn't want anything to do with him. Raphael said he'd be fine with that so long as he didn't hurt anyone.

"There's nothing he can hurt me with from where he is. He's already done the most damage to us that he could do by killing Momma. I'll only give him information that I feel he needs, which isn't going to be much. I'll tell him that Grandma has passed on, and that's about it on that score. I'll make myself a list before Thursday of things I won't talk to him about, so I don't forget. But he's not going to get any information about the sale or how we're doing now that we've sold the farm."

After his family left him, leaving behind Meggie, they talked about the list he was going to make up. With his right hand being cast up, she did help him in writing things down. It was starting to pain him a bit more, so they gave him something for it, and after that, he dozed for a bit. Having his family around these last few hours made him realize just how lucky he'd been in that accident. And he'd never forget how lucky he'd been.

Chapter 8

Walton waited for his turn to talk on the phone. There were ten of them, and all of a sudden, they were all being used. He didn't know how that normally worked as he'd never had anyone to call before. But today he was going to call his oldest son, Kinsey. It still sounded like a girl's name to him, but he wasn't going to piss him off by having him change it to something more manly. It occurred to him that he didn't have any kids named after himself, and that bothered him. He did wonder why his wife would do him dirty like that.

He had a list of things that he was going to ask his boy for. First and foremost, he wanted to know if any of them had taken after him and were any good at cards. He'd never been, but perhaps it skipped a family around, and he was the only one with the bad seed. Stepping up in line, he was the next one to go until it was his turn.

Money was first on the list. He needed someone to put him some cash in his allowance so that he could buy him a bag of chips once in a while. He'd seen others have some, and he wanted them bad enough to steal them. He wouldn't; that would get him in confinement, and he didn't want that.

When it was his turn, he had to ask how to get the number to work. He'd never made a call in all the time he'd been imprisoned, so he had some difficulties getting the phone operator to call someone for him. Kinsey said he'd take the call, and he nearly jumped around he was so happy that he'd be able to talk to someone besides himself.

"There are things that I'm not going to discuss with you, and one of them is money." As soon as he was on the phone, his kid started spouting off the things he was going to do or not. Walton told him he was his father and he'd talk to him about what he wanted. "You go on ahead and talk about it, then I'll hang up. And then change my number so that you can't ever call me again. Not that I want you to, but today we're going to see how things go. No money."

"But I have me a need for just a few bucks in my pot. That way I can get me some chips like I want." He didn't say a word. "We'll come back around to that then. I want to know how you guys are doing. Any of you coming up here to visit me?"

He realized then that he wanted to see his sons. All of them. And even if he had to be good for a month to get that, he knew he could do it just for the chance to see what he'd made. Six boys, men now. He'd made himself six kids and he was saddened by the fact that he didn't know a single one of them. He wouldn't even be able to pick them out of a lineup if his life depended on knowing one of them.

"We're not. We told you when you were in the courthouse that you're not to expect us to come see you, and I think that Grandma made it clear that we'd not be there either. What else did you want to know?" He asked about the others how they felt about coming to see him. "You're lucky in that I'm telling you that no one wants to see you. I don't believe that they'd be so nice about it."

That had him rubbing the part of his chest that he thought long dead, to being hurt by someone. His heart really did ache. He asked him about his mom, knowing that she had to have died by now, she'd always been old, but the boy didn't seem to want to tell him any details about her dying.

"She went to bed one night and didn't wake up. She's been gone about eight years now." He asked where she was buried. "Beside Grandda, where she wanted to be buried. What else?"

"Damn it, boy, don't you want to talk to me?" He said that he didn't, not really. "Well, that's too bad. I want to hear about things, and you're not telling me snot. Now, should I be expecting any of you to come up here in the system? It would do me a bit of good to be able to know that."

"Of course it would. Then we'd be no better than you are. None of us has been in trouble with the law. In fact, we've all served in the Army in some way and have come out better men than when we went in. We each have an education that has served us well." He asked about the youngest. "He's working at a job that he likes, all right. It pays the bills."

"What does he do? Maybe he has some way he can quit the job and come and see me. I'd like that." Kinsey told him that none of them were coming to see him. "You keep spouting that off. When was the last time you saw them that you could ask them? I'm betting you never see each other and you're just making that up."

"You and I are on speaker phone together, and they're all right here, but don't want to talk to you. If they wanted to, they could have by now." That hurt, too. Right there in the room, and they didn't want to say a word to him. That sucked. "They said if you know their names, they'll talk to you for a minute."

"Coyote or something like that." He didn't say a word. "His name is like that coyote that was on the cartoons when I was a kid. Forever fighting against the bird of some sort. That's his name, or close enough."

"No." Damn it all the fuck and back. He wanted someone to like him. He was their father after all. Then he heard one of them say that they'd talk to him, but he wasn't giving them his name.

"You can rot in there for all I care about you. You killed our momma when she did nothing wrong but to tell you no." He said he didn't much care for that word to be used around him. "Too bad. But I'll say it to you now, No, I don't want to ever have a thing to do with you again after today. I've been finished with you since you tried to get me to hold my momma down so that you could saw her head off."

"The police were coming, and I had to get rid of the body. If you ingrates would have helped, I might not have gotten so much jail time. Now, as it is, I have to be here forever. Don't that make any of you feel like you did me wrong?" It sounded to him like they all said no at the same time. "Ingrates. All of you are ingrates. Won't even come to see me like a good son would do. Put some money in my account so that I can have a bag of chips once in a while on my birthday. Do any of you even know when that is?"

"March seventh." Again, it sounded like they all said it at the same time, but only one of them spoke after that. "Do you have any idea when any of us were born? Or our names, for that matter? I'm betting not only do you not know, you more than likely have no idea what we look like. The color of our eyes or anything personal about us. I'm betting that no one ever called you a good father either. And they'd be right about that."

He stood there with the phone in his hand for a good two minutes before he realized that they'd hung up on him. He'd never got to talk to them about his list, nor did he have any idea what they did for money. Christ, it was like they all hated him or something. Putting the phone back on the handle, he walked away a broken man.

They treated him like he was dirt. Worse than that, it was like he'd not created him with his own body. Walton walked back to his room and laid on his cot. His heart was hurting him so badly right now, he was sure that it was breaking in his chest. Like he'd been popped there with a gun or something. Like he wasn't going to be all right again.

Supper was called, and he made his way to the dining room area. Looking at his food, all he could think about was that they didn't even care if he had some chips. What's a bag cost nowadays, a dime or something? One of them could have spared that much for their daddy. Wishing he'd not called them at all, he put his tray in the return shelf and went back to his room without touching a bit of it.

They'd been mean to him, and there was no call for it. It wasn't like he left them without anything. He'd not lost *all* the land for them. Momma had said they'd gotten it back for her. Well, he was the next in line and should have had enough for a bag of chips. He didn't even care what flavor they were right now.

"Pennington, your son called here right after you got off the phone with him. He said to tell you that you're not to call him again." He asked if he'd said anything about the chips. "Chips? No, he only said for you to not call again that they don't want to talk to you anymore."

"I don't want to talk to them anymore either. They were mean to me." The guard asked him what they'd done. "Wouldn't give me a lick of information about them. Not even to say about how they were doing. Said if I knew their names, I could talk to them for a bit."

"Did you know their names, Pennington?" He said that wasn't the point. "Sounds like it was to me. You have six sons, and you can't remember one of their names? That's terrible. You should have known at least the name of the kid that was in the accident, Coyote or something, didn't you say?"

"That's not his name—Wylie. Like the coyote. Wylie Coyote was his name." He asked if he'd called him that. "No, it's not Coyote either. Damn it, why should I have paid attention to their names when I'm their father? It's not that big of a deal if you asked me."

"I believe it was to them." He moved on, and

Walton told himself that he didn't care anymore. That he'd not eat any chips if they were to bring them to him themselves. He didn't care if he ever saw them either. Damned ingrates.

"I hope they all get the clap and die." He didn't want that either, he told himself. "Well, you'd think that a one of them would have felt a little sorry for their old man and gotten him a quarter or two in his pot. It would have been a bit to get me some chips."

He didn't know why he was so obsessed with chips. He didn't normally care for snack food. Especially chips. It was the principle of the thing. He deserved them, and they should have wanted him to have them.

"Instead, they have to act like I didn't have a part in them being alive, like I had nothing to do with it." He thought of all the things that he could have gotten if they'd just put a couple of bucks in his pot. "Like I know what I can buy. I don't want your money anyway, you little bastards. You're nothing but little bastards."

Walton wanted to be pissy with someone, to start a fight with one of the younger bloods that were still in the dining room. But he didn't. He wasn't nearly as stupid as people believed him to be. Being an old man like he was, there was no way he could match himself up with the kids that were in prison nowadays. They were not just smarter than him but more than likely knew ways to kill him that wouldn't require a gun or a knife. No, he wasn't going to be messing with them kids out there.

Thinking about how old he was, it took him nearly too long to figure it out, and he lost interest in what he'd been thinking about. The nearest that he could figure was that he was nearly seventy years old or thereabouts. He might well have been older, but certainly no younger than that. It made him sort of sick to his belly when he thought of being ninety years old someday and still being in prison for a crime that had been pushed on him by his wife.

"Damn her. She should have said yes to me." He tried to remember what he'd wanted her to say yes to, but it was all confusing with the thoughts of how old he was. Then he thought about how his boys should have done right by him, and they'd not. "What did we even have them for if they were going to be treating me like this when I needed them most?"

At lights out, he was on his cot but not ready to sleep. So long as he wasn't causing any trouble, they didn't care if he slept or not. So long as he wasn't bothering the other inmates, he didn't have to sleep. Instead, he decided to write a letter to his boys, at least to the girly-sounding one. Walton didn't spell all that well, but he knew what he wanted to say. He was going to be putting down the law to them, and they'd listen by god. Damned ingrates.

After three hours of just trying to spell the boy's name, he gave up. There wasn't no point in him writing to him if he didn't know how to spell his name. In fact, he wondered if any of them knew his name. That would have been a kicker, them bitching about him not knowing their names when they didn't even know his. Getting into his cot, he thought of all the times that he'd been home with the kids and never bothered with them.

"They're lucky that I didn't beat them all to death when I had the chance." He wouldn't have done that. He never once hit them. Or Martha, for that matter, until that night. "I'm more of a gambling man than a beater. They should have known that about me."

It did get him to thinking about how much they knew about him. He'd never been home all that much, and when he was there, he never bothered with any of them. He'd been looking for his next big stake and how he was going to win all the money in a good game of poker or whatever other card game was going on. Hell, he would have played *Go Fish* if there was any money involved. Now that he thought on it, he really had been in prison or jail more than he'd been at home. Laughing slightly to himself, he thought that should have made him Father of the Year for them. He'd never disciplined them, nor had he touched them once in any kind of harmful way. They should have figured out that he was the best daddy in the world for all that he'd done for them by being in jail all the time.

"Damned ingrates. Didn't even realize how good they had it made until now. I should have told them that when I had them on the phone. Kids? Who needed them." He fell asleep knowing that he'd been a good dad to his kids, not like some of the others in here. He'd not tell them that, of course. That was his own good story that he was going to keep for himself. "Yes, sir. I was the best, and they should have known that."

~*~

David watched Kinsey sleeping. They said he'd had a rough night with bad dreams. He'd had few himself about the accident and wouldn't want anyone to know how badly the thing had bothered him. He looked around the room that Kinsey had for himself.

He hadn't always been a good man, not like he was today. If it hadn't been for his wife, he might well have gone on being a bully and a bastard. But she told him that she'd not marry him if he was going to act like a child without a nap, and that had him changing things around, not at first, of course. But he'd learned his lesson when he'd ended up on the wrong end of a gun and it had nearly killed him. David had learned really fast that he was headed down the wrong path in his life, and it would surely get him killed.

"You learn anything from this?" He was lying in a hospital bed with all kinds of tubes coming out of him when he'd been shot three times in his chest. "I won't be back if you ever pick up a gun or knife again to settle your problems."

David couldn't even talk to her; another machine was keeping him alive. Nodding his head once, he hoped that she'd understand that he was going to keep right on being what he was and there wasn't anything she could do about it. But she misunderstood him.

"Do you have any idea what my dad did to keep you out of prison? He had to call in favors from all over the world so that you could marry me someday. If you still want that?" Again, he nodded, but he was determined not to be a changed man because she wanted him to. "I won't put up with you doing things by your own hand anymore, David Winchester. I'm a good woman, and you'd be better off if you were to do what I tell you and live. I would have no problem pulling the plug on you the next time."

Turns out she'd been asked to do that when he'd been brought in. The diamond on her finger had given her a lot of rights that week. One of them being the one who decided if he lived or not. He was really glad that she'd been in a better mood than she'd been in when he finally woke up. She got right in his face.

"You have one week to get your affairs in order, or I'll order a hit on you that won't miss this time. And if I'm given the chance, I'll pull that plug and see you dead before I'll have my name associated with you being a monster. Do you understand me? I'll do it too." He had no doubt that she would, and it frightened him a great deal that she would have him killed by someone better than the man who had tried. "One week to get your shit together, or I'm going to do it too. And it won't matter if I go to jail or not. My dad has a lot more favors he could pull in for me, and see you six feet under and me living my life without you."

After that talk, he never so much as touched a gun, only to have them sold from his house and every one of them out of his house. He made amends to those that he'd wronged, and there were a lot of them, and spent the next fifty years or so being married to a woman that kept him on the straight and narrow and never once gave him reason to not love her. When they found out that his youth had cost him the ability to have children, she stayed with him then, too. David knew that he was a lucky man and knew that for the rest of his life, he'd love the woman who had threatened him with certain death if he didn't get his shit together. Now he was looking in on a man that he would have loved to have fathered had he been given the chance.

"What are you doing here? Don't you have some other farmer that you could pester?" He told Kinsey that he didn't, he'd had enough of that for one lifetime. "Good. You're kind of growing on me, and I like having you around."

"I've been wondering when you're going to get to go home." Kinsey laughed a little and stopped when the pain got to him. The boy was in a great deal of pain, and the contusion from his armpit to his hip bone was testament to how much he'd done to save himself and his brother. "There are some things that I wanted to talk to you about now that you're going to be all right for the next fifty years."

"They said that I could possibly go home on Tuesday. I just have to be able to move a bit better. My leg is giving me the most pain. They said that my ankle was turned up under the clutch, and it bruised it all the way to the bone." He said that they'd told him he was lucky that he'd not broken his ankle. "I think I'm lucky on a lot of fronts about that accident. More than I would have ever thought when I was sitting in the truck with the police all around."

"Wylie went home yesterday, as you know. He's been looking at houses around the town. It's been put out there that you've sold the land now, and people are clamoring to get to see the six of you to see if you'll spend a bit of your money on them." He said that he needed to get him a house, too, if he was going to be living somewhere besides a hotel when he got out. "I have that taken care of. You and Meggie are going to be staying with my wife and I until you can get around enough to purchase yourself a home. She's thinking that you should build, and I don't blame her. There aren't enough houses in your town for a man with as much money as you have."

"I can live anywhere." Sitting him up a bit better hurt him in ways that he didn't explain to the younger man because he couldn't stand for him to hurt. "I know that you've demolished the old house by now, haven't you?"

"I have. They started construction on the new house last week." It seemed that every day they were finding things that were wrong with Kinsey, and it hurt his heart that he'd not tried harder to get him to ride in the limo with him. But as Wylie had explained, someone would have been hit by the semi, and they might not have survived like the two of them had. "You'll live in the big house with Alice and me, and we'll take care of you."

"You know that I can pretty much take care of myself." He asked him how he was going to do that when he couldn't even piss without help. "I'll figure it out."

"I think Meggie likes the idea of living in the

big house with us. She said she should have thought about you not being able to get around as well when she suggested her house to live in. Ours is all one floor, but for the wine cellar, and you don't drink, so that's not an issue. Besides, you'll be getting around sooner rather than later."

"I know, but I don't want to put you out." He promised him that he wasn't doing that at all. "What does Alice think about having a grown man around the house that can barely feed himself, much less piss? I bet you've talked her into it."

"You'd be surprised to know that this was her idea. Not to mention, when you get to know her better, you'll see that nothing happens that she doesn't approve of before I say a word. She's kept me out of enough scrapes since I married her that I know when to keep my mouth shut and do as I'm told. You'd be well to remember that when you're all settled in the house with us." David thought about all the things they'd talked about since Kinsey was brought into their lives, like he'd been. "It's all settled. Once you're free to leave here, we have a live-in nurse who will take care of all the necessary things you have to do in the bathroom taken care of. Also, she'll be able to do your physical therapy too. I'm to understand that you're going to need a bit of that."

"I hurt myself." Which was an understatement

if he'd ever heard of. Most of the boy's body had been hurt in some way, and he was luckier than he'd thought. Not only could he have been cut in half, but he would have lost him that day, and he hated to think about that. "I'd do it all again to save us, but I surely do hurt a great deal now that I have. Who would have thought that I'd be here for all this time because I was in an accident?"

"Anyone that looks at you would have known it wasn't just an accident, but a god-awful, terrible, horrific accident that nearly took you both from us." He didn't want to talk about it, so he changed the subject. "Alice and Meggie with Grace are out shopping. Since you didn't have much in the way of clothing when we packed you out of the house, they decided to go and get you things that you could wear around the house when you get there. Did you even own a pair of slippers?"

"I didn't have any use for them. I'd get out of bed and dress for the day after a shower, then go to bed when I undressed for the evening. If my feet got cold, I'd simply put on an extra pair of socks. I don't even own a robe." He said that he knew that, too. "You seem to know a great deal about my clothing habits. What's all this about?"

"I want to tell you something. Something that I've never told another being in my life." He looked at the young man and felt the tears fill his eyes. "I love you like you were my son, Kinsey. Your brothers, too, though not to the same extent. They're…you're all good men, and you make me want to be good too. I know that sounds sappy, but it would give me the greatest pleasure on earth if you were to treat me like the father you never had."

"I don't know what to say." He took his hand into his and held it. "You've been like a father to me since I met you. Every decision I've made since meeting you has been in the form of what you would say if I were to have asked you about it."

"I do the same thing when I think of what I'm doing. Even Alice has said that I've become a changed man since you came into my life." He pulled his hand away and blew his nose. "I'm getting too old for sentimentalism. It gets me in the feels if you want to know the truth."

"I feel the same way." As they sat there talking, he could tell that Kinsey wanted something for the pain. It hurt him that the younger man could barely sit up without being sick with the pain of it. But the doctor told them all that in a few days, he'd be better at sitting up and even standing. When he stood up, on his own, he'd be able to go home on Tuesday, and they'd be able to pamper him at home all they wanted.

"Let me get the nurse for you." Kinsey said

he'd be all right for a little bit; he wanted to talk to him about this house that he was moving into. "It's a nice little ranch style with eight bedrooms. You'll be taking up one of them for your room with Meggie, and then one of them will be set up for your therapy. Like the doctor said to you, once you start getting up on your own, things will feel better for you. Especially walking around. He said that once you get your feet under you, things will start to feel like they're back in place and you'll feel better about eating and everything else, too."

"I'll be happy when I can eat better food. This soft stuff is for the birds." He laughed a little, and David could see what it cost him. "I'll be working on getting better so we don't push you out of your home, David. Meggie and I appreciate everything you've done for us."

"To be honest with you, Kinsey, we've enjoyed having someone to care for. We've not had anyone to pamper since we got married, and we're having fun." As soon as he got him situated in the bed, he called the nurse in. He'd only wanted about half of the pain meds, and David was happy for that. The sooner he was off those drugs, the better off he'd be, too.

Chapter 9

"May I walk with you, Kinsey?" He'd been walking the house since he'd been able to get out of the bed. It hurt those first few days, and he didn't think he was ever going to get better. But here he was walking with just a cane and doing pretty good if he did say so himself. "I've been wondering something since you got home. Did the doctors tell you why you were so bruised up? I mean, you seemed to be in fit shape before all this, and you were black and blue all over yourself."

"He said it was because I was tense when it happened. And so tense afterwards that my body couldn't handle anymore strain put on it. So everything that touched me or people touched me, it left a bruise. He said that was the only thing he could think of for me, looking like I did. It was that or I was rolled under the tire a few times and someone didn't tell me." He watched himself carefully when he went up the little stair that led to the dining room. "I have to be careful about everything until I get used to things. A tiny stair like that could send me to the hospital again. Not really, but I am careful of everything. But I promise you I'm getting better every day."

"I know you are, son. I can see it on you." She walked with him from the dining room through the living room into the den. It was his routine to do it three times a day until he was able to do it without thinking about every little dust bunny. "Meggie is working today, I take it. She's usually with you on these long ventures of yours. It's like a treat from me to get to do it with you."

"She only goes in two days a week now. As soon as I'm better, she'll drop down to one. So we can get to know one another again. It's been physical therapy on top of physical therapy since I've been home." Alice said that he was getting better about that, too. "Yeah, well, Meggie had a talk with me, and she scared me a bit. Not physically, but I'm not going to complain as much when they come to make me stretch out."

They both laughed, and he thought it was funny that he really had been afraid of Meggie a bit. When she started telling him that if he didn't want to get better, why did he save himself for her, he took it more seriously. He didn't know what he'd do without her in his life right now. Or anytime for that matter. While he was down too, she'd been teaching him how to invest with his money. Christ, every time he thought of how much money he had, it would give him the willies.

"Our house is coming along nicely. I noticed that

your brothers are doing well, too." Wylie had built him a house, but the others had purchased one. And they'd all gotten themselves something to drive around in that while wasn't brand new, but it was newer than the one they'd been using on the farm. He shivered whenever he thought of that old truck. "Have you and Meggie decided what you want to do yet? I know it's not been that long since you've been looking, but I thought that you guys were set to live in her house."

"We've decided that we want children someday, and if we live in her house, it will cost us more for upgrades than it will to just get something new. And that includes building. There are only two bathrooms in her old house, and that's not enough with kids in the house. At least that's what she tells me. The old house we lived in only had one, and there were eight of us living there at one time with my grandparents. So I'm leaving that part up to her knowledge." He sat back down in the chair that had been purchased for him to use in the living room. It was a workout chair that he could do leg lifts with, as well as tone up his arms. "May I ask you why you're building such a big house? I thought you'd be downsizing instead of building bigger."

"Me too. I thought a lot of things, but David wants to entertain again. We've not done that in years. So when he gets a burr up his bottom, I let him have his way. It's that or he does that pouty thing with his lip, and I can't stand that." Kinsey laughed when she did. He'd noticed that pouty thing too. "But the house does have things in it that are going to make it easier for us when we get older. The master bedroom is on the lower floor, and there is a spa just off the master that will be nice for old bones and tired muscles. I'm not saying that I'm old, but I'm going to be using that room a great deal when we get moved in."

"Sounds nice. The house that we had been looking at had one of those spa pools that is big enough to swim in, and the current is whatever you want to set it at. But the rest of the house needed major work, and we passed up on that one." He lifted his legs up with the weights on them and did that ten times before he upped the amount of weights. "Have you decided what to do with this house? David seemed like he wasn't going to be happy selling it off."

"That's something that I wanted to talk to you and Meggie about. We'd like for you two to live in this house for us." He nearly dropped the weight he was using on his foot. "I know that it's a big house. Lord, I can't believe how big this house is at times, but it would be perfect for your growing family someday, and it's perfectly situated between where your brothers are living. I think it's less than ten miles from Wylie's home. And only a few minutes more until you get to

Gleason's home. We love for you to have it."

"It's a wonderful home and I love it here. But that's something that I'd have to talk over with Meggie. Do you think that it's in our budget?" She said that they'd make sure that it was. "We wouldn't want you to take a loss on the house just for us. You can't stay rich doing things like that."

"I know for a fact that it's in your budget, and we'll all talk when you talk to Meggie." She looked up when one of the housemaids came into the room. There was a phone call for her. "Well, I should get that. You two talk it over and let us know. David will be back this evening for dinner, and we can answer any of your questions then." She stood up, and he had to fight hard not to do the same when she stood. "I love you, Kinsey. Both you and Meggie so very much."

Then she was gone. Glancing at the clock, he knew that Meggie would be home in another hour, and he still had two hours of exercise to do yet. Another thing that he had to be careful with was overdoing it. He had the first couple of days, and that set him back for a week. So he did what he was supposed to in the allotted time that he set up for himself, and that was all. No more thinking that he was Superman and could leap over small or large buildings simply because he wanted to by now.

After he was finished and Meggie was home,

she helped him with the arm weights, and the two of them talked about the house. She said that she thought that was what David had planned the other night when he was hinting about it, but of course, he'd not gotten that. Sometimes he thought he was dense on top of being hurt. He never caught the little hints that David and Alice would hint to him about things, like the pool.

He'd been able to use the pool, but hadn't because a pool sounded like it was something personal to a person, like hot bath water. He'd never get into the bath before his brothers did, just because that was gross. He didn't want to gross up another family's pool. But David had told him that he had a lift put on the pool so that people with injuries could easily get in and out of it. There were other hints, too, but he'd not gotten those either.

So he asked David straight up if he could use the pool. The man looked at him like he was crazy and told him that was why he'd had the lift put in. Just for him to use. And now there were the house hints that he'd never got. He supposed that was why Alice came straight out and told him about it. He never seemed to understand when people were doing things for him.

"I want to talk to you about sex, too." He looked around to see if anyone was around. He was embarrassed that Meggie was so free with what she said at times, not at her but for himself. Kinsey supposed that had to do with being around his grandparents most of his life. They never talked about anything like that or even hinted. Not that he ever got any hints that was. "What are you going to do when one of our kids wants to get advice about sex?"

"Oh, that's easy, I'm going to tell them to go ask Mom." She smacked him on the arm and laughed with him. "It's just that I don't want anyone to think that we're having sex in their home."

"I'm pretty sure when they said we could have the same bedroom, they knew that eventually we'd be having sex. I've spoken to your doctor like you asked me to do, and he said so long as you don't try to do any barrel rolls or swing from the light fixtures, we should be all right. We just have to be careful not to do anything too fast or strenuous." He said that having sex with her was strenuous. "Good. I was hoping you were up to this. I miss you."

"I miss you, too." They kissed, and he could feel his cock getting the better of him. Since he was only wearing sweatpants so that he could get in and out of them more easily to go to the bathroom, he had to adjust himself twice before he pulled away. "I think that we should talk about other things, too, besides sex." She tsked at him. "I want you to marry me. If you would. I mean, would you marry me?"

"That was so romantic. Wanna try again?" He nodded and told her that while he couldn't get down on one knee yet, for her to imagine him there. "All right. I have that image in my head. What do you have to say to me, big boy?"

"I've messed up a few times with this relationship. We're so different, and I think that's what makes me love you so much. You're going to be keeping me guessing all the time. I want that every day of the rest of my life with you. If you'll have me. Meggie Gold, will you consent to be my wife and put up with me daily? Keep me on my toes and love me until the end of time?" She told him no, she'd love him beyond the end of time. "I love you. You nearly gave me a heart attack when you said no, but I understand that. I have a ring."

"You do? How on earth did you manage that? I know for a fact that you've not gone anywhere yet." He fumbled in his pants for a few seconds before he pulled out the little blue box. "Oh, Kinsey, you really did have a ring for me."

"I wish I could tell you that I went to the store and found this on my own for you, but your grandma did it for me. She and I had an open line that she showed me all the rings, and I found that one, but without her help, I'd have to make you a promise of a ring. I hope you like this one." He opened the little box and pulled on the diamond engagement ring for his one and only true love. "It's pretty in the box, but I'm betting that it looks gorgeous on your hand."

It did look good on her hand and even better when she held it up to the light and let the diamonds sparkle off the fireplace that was lit in difference to the chill in the air. He loved that most of the rooms had their own gas fireplace, but he loved too how romantic he could be with her in the room with him. Kissing her again, he reminded her that he needed an answer to his question.

"Yes, yes, forever I'll be your wife." She kissed him several times all over his face, and she then carefully got onto his lap. "Wanna go to bed with me?"

"I'd love to, but we're having dinner with David and Alice tonight. It's about the house." She did the pouty thing with her lips, too, but it was cute on her while on David, it made him look like an old man with a swollen lip. "I love you."

Almost as if they'd shouted for them, David and Alice came into the room just as he was trying to figure out if one told the people they were living with that he'd just proposed to Meggie. But again, Meggie took that right to them and they were congratulating them.

"This calls for some champagne. I have just the bottle that we can use too." David sent one of the housemaids to the cellar for the wine, and someone else went to get glasses. He'd never had servants before, but if he ever did, he'd treat them like Alice and David treated them. Like they were a part of the household, too. They had glasses of champagne too. "Now that you've finally popped the question and said yes, we might as well talk about this house. We'd like for the two of you to take it off our hands. You're close enough to your families and love this house as much as we do. So I'm going to go down to the bank on Monday morning and put your names on the deed."

"Wait, we have to talk about financing and stuff." Kinsey didn't know what the stuff would involve, but he knew that there had to be some. Meggie put her hand on his leg. "I've missed something again, haven't I?"

"They want to give us the house, I think?" David and Alice both nodded. "And in doing so, we'll live here in this house and make it our forever home. Right?"

"I've been trying to tell the two of you for the past week that's what I wanted to do. Kinsey, you're going to have to pay attention to me or you might well miss out on some things. Anyway, we have also talked it over and we want to adopt the two of you, too. Not really adopt with the paperwork and all, but we've already done it in our hearts. We've loved you since the first time that we met the two of you, and can't think of anyone else who would put up with us the way that you guys have. We're moving you around like your little pegs on a board, so to speak." David looked at his wife and smiled. "I'm not doing this correctly, am I?"

"I think you're doing just fine, but then I've known you all my life, it feels like." She sat down on the couch when David did. "What he's trying to hard to tell you is that we've never had children, but if we had, we'd want them to be just like the two of you. You're not perfect, but we love you anyway. And we'd like for you to take this house. We're not going to be happy with anyone else living here but the two of you, and that's the way it should be. The contractors said that our house will be ready in a few weeks. And in that time, you can start making this place your own. We know you don't have much of your own, so we're leaving things behind that we don't want to take with us. Which is pretty much everything. We're starting fresh, and you two can do the same with this place."

"I don't know what to say." David told him to say yes. "There's a lot to think about. Not just the house, but you guys not being here anymore. I don't know if I can stand that or not."

"Oh, Kinsey, I do love you, son. You couldn't have said anything better than that about us leaving you here on your own." David poured them more of the bubbly and toasted them and the house. "I hope you have us tiny little versions of yourself so that we can spoil them like grandparents and have dates with them when they're older, too."

The rest of the evening and into dinner, they talked about the wedding. Neither of them wanted a big wedding, and the courthouse would do them just fine, but David wanted a huge wedding with all the bells and whistles. They were going to talk more about that as soon as Kinsey was able to get up and around better. But for now, they were going to take the house as it had meant so much to them getting him better and carving out a suite just for her grannie so she could continue to live with her and Kinsey.

As they made their way to bed, they didn't talk much about the day. Kinsey was nervous about having sex with Meggie. Not enough not to try, but with the pain still so fresh in his mind, he knew that he was in for a challenge of his life tonight and wanted more than anything to please Meggie. He only hoped that he didn't hurt himself in the process. He loved her so much.

~*~

Meggie was nervous about having sex with Kinsey. Several times a day, she would close her eyes when she thought of how badly he looked in the hospital. And how much pain he'd been in. Tonight was going to go slowly, and she was going to make sure that he had as much pleasure as she could give him without killing him. Smiling to herself, she did wonder what he was thinking about.

"I have to admit I'm looking forward to this." She laughed, telling him she hoped he was. "I mean, I was very afraid of it a week ago. The thought of how much we enjoyed ourselves the first time, and I wonder how we survived it. We couldn't do anything like that now, or we would hurt me."

"I don't ever want to see you hurt like that again. You mean too much to me." The two of them got into bed, and he pulled his sweatpants off. He'd been wearing the bottoms to pajamas, and she the top, but he didn't bother with it tonight. He wanted her and was going to show her the best way he knew how.

Rolling to his side, he pulled Meggie to his body. They'd been sleeping this way for the last few weeks when he was able to take the pressure of lying on his side, that is. When she moved her ass back against his cock he felt himself grow hard, then harder still. Putting his hand on her breast, he moaned when her nipple hardened under his fingers. She moved her ass again, and he nearly came up off the bed when she reached around to his cock and held him.

"This is nice." He thought so too, but was having a hard time forming words. It had been a few months, and he was still just a little afraid. "I love the way you fill my hand, Kinsey. You're so full right now that I bet if I were to take you in my mouth, you'd fuck me hard."

"Yes, sweetheart. I need to feel you at my cock." She adjusted around so that she was facing him. When he rolled to his back at her request, he was surprised and thrilled when she sat upon him with her legs on either side of him. He could feel his cock leaking when she reached down and adjusted him for her own pleasure. "I want to fuck you."

"Yes, in a minute. I want to feel you right here." She rode him, riding him slowly, just made it all the better. "It's been so long, Kinsey, I nearly forgot how large you were."

While she rode his cock, he reached up and filled his hands with her breasts. They were full, too; her nipples were hard and sticking right out from her breasts like a beacon begging him for his mouth.

Sitting up a little, he pulled the shirt off she had on and was happy for the little bounce her breasts did. Lifting them up, he suckled first one then the other while she pulled his briefs off his swollen cock and played with the crown. As she adjusted herself around, he cried out when she impaled herself onto his cock and didn't move. He pulled her body closer to his and held her there while his body, his cock adjusted to this new thing. Rolling to her side, she took him with her, and he held himself upward so as not to crush her.

"Take me." He moved his hips, careful not to hurt her too. "More, Kinsey. I need more of you."

Making love to her wasn't nearly as hard as he thought it would be. Taking her hands above her head and holding them there, he ran his free hand down her arms and to her breasts. They responded just as he had hoped they would and swelled more into his hand while he made his way down her throat to her full breast.

Moving down to her hips, he pulled her groin closer to his as he made a downward thrust. Having her meet him was like having her just where he wanted her. As her legs lifted up and wrapped around his hips, Kinsey nearly came when she cried out with her first release.

"More baby. I want to feel more from you." She came twice more at his encouragement, demanding that she come for him until he felt the first stirring of her coming again. As she rose up to meet him again, he plunged deep inside of her and released. His entire body tensed up until he felt his cum coming from his toes.

Drained, he knew that he was going to pass out and didn't care. As he held onto Meggie, holding her and fucking her through one more climax, his arms fell away, and he closed his eyes. There was nothing like having great sex, then passing out.

When he woke, she was still atop him. He groaned a little when she moved, but they stayed the way that they were. Meggie lifted her head to her hand and looked down at him. She had the most beautiful smile on her face that he'd ever seen.

"I hope we created a child tonight." He'd forgotten a condom. "I don't care if we create fifty babies tonight, I'm so in love with you that I only want what you want. Children."

"We never really talked about how many. I think fifty is more than I think either of us can handle, not to mention, babysitting would cost us a fortune." She laughed like he hoped that she did. Moving her hair from her cheek, he realized how good it felt to be able to tell her that he loved her. "You're everything that I didn't know I wanted in a wife. We'll figure out the domestic stuff later. Right now, I want to bask in your love."

"If we did create a child, we'd mess up David's plans of a giant wedding." He said there was that. "Also, we need to make plans about this house. I want to make it ours instead of living in their shadow."

"I agree. The first thing we need to do is upgrade the kitchen. I can't believe how outdated it is." Moving his leg, he was careful of his ankle. It still bothered him at times if he wasn't careful. "Then the master bedroom. We should make it a priority." She said all the bedrooms would need to be upgraded. "I agree with you there."

They made love again, and he thought it was the most romantic thing they'd ever done. It was soft and gentle, but it was good too. They took their time exploring each other's bodies and made sure that they each got the most pleasure out of their lovemaking as they could. He loved this woman and knew that he would for the rest of his life. Finally, when they went to sleep, he held her tightly in his arms as she softly snored her rest with him.

Getting up while the room was still dark, he made his way to the bathroom. Not making too much noise, he flushed and washed his hands. As he was going back to bed, he nearly screamed when Meggie came toward him. He didn't know who else would be in the room with him but her, but it was something he'd not been expecting. As soon as he was back under the covers, she joined him in the bed again, and he pulled her to him. She complained about him being too cold, but she was warm, so he made her lie still with him. Laughing to himself, he told her that he'd be warm in a minute.

When he woke again, he was alone in the big bed. Her side was still warm, so he knew she'd not gone far. When she came out of the closet, the sucker was big enough for both their clothes, she was dressed for the office. She sat on the side of the bed with him and told him where she was going.

"There is a mess going on with the merger that is supposed to be going on next week. The elderly man wants to back out now that he realizes that the younger man is going to tear his company office up and make it more modern." He asked her if that was normal to do that to an old company. "It's the only way that it's going to survive, and the influx of cash will keep it open until all the renovations are finished."

"So he doesn't like that his company isn't going to be the one that he went to every day." She told him that was it exactly. "I feel sorry for the older man. It's not that he doesn't like change, I mean, he did go into this merger with his eyes wide open, but starting with the offices might not be the way to go right away. I mean, that's just me."

"What would you do first? I mean, a great deal has to depend on the offices being redone so that the transit part can get started. It's not important that it be done immediately." He told her what he'd do. "The bathrooms do need to be upgraded, too. But I can see what you mean, it will be a promise of bigger things coming to the company, instead of starting out with the most mess and going from there."

"Unless he has a thing for the bathrooms being

the way that they are. I don't know the man. Then I'd work on the breakrooms if there are any. If not, then put some in. That will tell the people working in the building that he cares for them, too. It's not much, but it might go a long way in making sure that everyone is on the same page when everything is getting done."

"I like that. Getting them all to feel like they're a part of the merger will help with morale when things start getting very messy with the reconstruction going on. That's a brilliant idea." She started to stand and looked at him. "Want to come with me? I know you've not been out of the house since we moved in, and it might be fun for you to get out and about."

"I don't have to drive, do I?" She asked him why that would matter. "I'm not sure I can just yet. Every time I think about getting behind the wheel, I have a nervous breakdown. Seriously, it might take me a while to get back to driving."

"Then that is something that we'll work on later." She kissed him on the cheek and told him to get ready. "We can take this slow, too. But you really need to get out of the house. You're beginning to smell like old socks."

Laughing, he got dressed. He didn't have any jeans here, but he did have some new dresser pants to wear. Pulling a shirt over his head, he realized how much weight he'd lost and would work on that too.

He'd never been a thin man, but he had been buffed up. It was from working all day on the farm and with the cattle. Yes, he thought, he needed to get in better shape all the way around his body.

Chapter 10

Wylie hated his house. He had been all right moving into it, but spending a month getting used to living alone and in the place made him realize that he didn't care for it. There was so much more that he needed than just four walls and a toilet. That wasn't all he had, but it felt like it when he had to stop and think every time where he was going in the place. It was laid out all wrong.

Standing in the hallway that divided the living room and the dining room, he realized that the hall was what was messing with him. There were no decorations on it, and it was a bit too narrow. Like it had been put in as an afterthought. He'd had pictures on the walls when he'd moved in, but had to remove them when he kept knocking them off the wall every time he came down the stupid thing. It wasn't necessary to the flow of the house. And it was a dead end at the very end.

"What are you doing?" He'd forgotten that Raphael had spent the night last night. "If you're going to bitch about the endless hallway, I'm leaving. I don't see anything wrong with it. Other than it's too narrow for men our size, and that it seems out of place to the rest of the house. You know, you're right, it is the worst place to put a hall. It only goes from the dining room to the living room. Why not just leave it open instead of putting up more walls?"

"That's just what I was trying to tell you last night." He said he got it now. "What would happen if I were to tear these two walls out? Do you think the upstairs will come down on top of us?"

"Something about load-bearing walls. Is it one? I have no idea. That's out of my league. We could find someone to help with that, I'm sure." He said he'd have to spend money on that. "Yeah, but we have enough to do things like that. Wouldn't you rather know now, other than when the ceiling is coming down on our heads?" Wylie grinned and said it would more than likely make the bank happier. "Yes, there is that too. Tell me again why you took out a loan to buy this house?"

"To stimulate the economy or something like that. Meggie told me it's better for the town. I don't know. If they want to sell houses, they should let you rent them first to find out if it's a fit for you, rather than having to go through all this to find out if the wall will be able to be taken out." He looked at the ceiling. "I wonder if it's true that the upper floors depend on the walls down here? I can see it happening, but I wonder too. I find myself wondering about a lot of things lately."

"Me too, but mine is on buying things. Like, do I really need two packs of underwear when one is fine? Do I need both black and white socks now that I own a suit? That one has been driving me crazy. Also, and this is a biggy. Do I need to buy a house right now, or can I just get myself something like a condo? There are some nice ones in town. And if I don't like living in it, there are all kinds of houses to rent, like you said, I want a fit first." Wylie asked him if he had a place in mind to rent. "No. But that's only because I don't know how to rent anyplace that I might want to live. I thought about asking Meggie, but she'd just pop me in the back of the head and tell me what I need to do. I want to talk to someone first. Not be told what to do."

"She doesn't really do that, does she?" Raphael shook his head and said that the popping part he'd made up, but she would tell him what he should do. "I can see her doing that. But you know she only wants what's best for us. Right?"

"I get it. She's forever asking me if I need anything. I do, but not what she could offer me. I need someone to talk to. I thought about David." Wylie said he'd be a good one to talk to. "Yeah, I think so too. Not that Meggie wouldn't listen, but she's so stressed out about Kinsey, too, and her job. I don't think she likes her job all that much, do you?"

"No. I think you're right there. She seems to spend a lot of time hanging out with our brother. Which I can understand, they love each other. But she's really worried about him all the time." He was too until he saw him walking around. That sort of set him up to thinking that his brother was getting better and not getting worse. "I'll never forget that truck accident. I wonder what the attorney David hired is going to be doing about it?"

Wylie had purchased himself a car. No one could drive the truck anymore, and he had been getting tired of walking everywhere he wanted to go. So when they had speculated about the house as much as they could and the falling down upstairs, they decided to have lunch. He was careful with his money and not eating out all the time, but it sure made it easier when he just wanted a meal without having to fix one for himself. David was in the place with Kinsey.

"We were just talking about the two of you. Well, all of you guys, but we did mention you too specifically. Are you still renting out the hotel on a weekly payment plan, Raphael?" He said he'd been thinking of getting a condo until he could figure out how to live by himself. "Good plan that. Then keep it when you decide and rent it out. That'll be a nice income for you."

Wylie smiled. And just like that, Raphael had the advice needed without any fuss or head popping. He asked him about his wall problem. David said that it would structurally have the house falling in.

"Not all at once, but if it's a load-bearing wall, then over time the upper walls will come down a bit more all the time until one day it will just happen. But like I said, not all at once. Are you sure it's a load-bearing wall?" He said he wasn't sure but didn't know how to tell. "I have a buddy of mine who can tell you about it. You do know that if you don't like the house you're living in, you need to get out before it sours you on all houses. You'll be comparing all homes to that one, and you'll never find a place to live. But don't sell it, like your brother, rent it out. Renters don't fuss much about a wall or not if they're getting a good price. I'll have my attorney go over your options about rental agreements before you get that far."

He wished he'd come to David before he purchased his first home. But he liked the idea of renting it out. Having income coming in could never hurt, but he'd be a good landlord, not one who wouldn't fix anything. That was the most common complaint of his friends who had rentals. That nothing was ever fixed.

They enjoyed their lunch together with Kinsey and David. David picked up the check, which was nice, and they all had some fun. Kinsey was looking good; he had on some pants today with a nice polo shirt that looked good on him, and he was glad to see that he was still using the cane. Every time he had to think about the accident, he would think of his brother saving his life. He had too.

After lunch they all went house hunting together. It was fun with David and Kinsey. He was getting good at spending his money for investment purposes David told them and he was proud of his brother once again.

"Finding yourself a fixer-upper is both a good thing and a bad thing. You have to balance how much you're going to have to spend to get it back up to where people will want to live in it and how much you will have to charge them to live there. All the fixing in the world won't help the area that a rental is in. You have to take that into consideration, too." Kinsey said that Meggie had told him that. "I'm looking for a rental that can be used for office space. But I'm not opposed to paying for it if it's in the perfect spot. I'm going to be working with some of the farmers around town to help with their animals. Not a vet, not yet anyway, but I need something to do that doesn't involve farming to the extent that we were doing it to before."

"Don't you have like a million rooms at your house?" He'd been so happy that David had given the house to his brother for him and Meggie to live in. It was the type of house that he wanted. All one floor and big enough to spread around in. His brother told him why he was looking for space. "I can see that. Not bringing your work home with you or having it there would be a problem if you just wanted to step away. Good idea. How big are you looking?"

"I don't want it to be too big, then I'll just be roaming the halls like I am at home. But something big enough that I can spread out if I want to." That too made sense to him. Wylie didn't think he was stupid, but he was learning a great deal about things on this trip. "Meggie has decided to quit her job and have someone else run it. She wants to work only a few days a month instead of every day. I'm happy about that."

They spent the day together, the four of them. Wylie finally got him a small notebook to make notes in so that he didn't fuck up again. He should have done what Raphael was doing and not bought the first house that he saw. He'd been stupid about that. But he'd been without a home right after the accident and had panicked. He wouldn't do that again. Careful planning would keep him in money, too.

By dinner time, they were all together still and eating at a nice restaurant. He'd been getting better about ordering in nicer restaurants by listening to David and his brothers. When they wanted steaks, they went to a steak house, and if you were at a seafood place, you didn't necessarily want to order steak. They might be better at the seafood. Like he thought before, he wasn't stupid, but he was a little naïve about how to get things to work for him. These bits and pieces of information were going to make him better at keeping his money, too.

Going home that night, he was happier than he'd been in a while. He'd made some major mistakes, but they were all ones that he could fix now before he started throwing money at them to get them fixed. He was all for getting a condo like his brother and maybe even sharing one—it wasn't as if they couldn't live together again. But he was going to be more careful with everything in his life, and he was doing that tonight.

Tomorrow he was going to talk to an attorney about different things that he'd had questions about. He'd never had this much money on a scale like this, and if he kept doing things by the seat of his pants, he was going to be broke again. He didn't want that feeling ever again.

David told him the secret to having money all the time was to balance it out with money coming in as it was going out. He didn't understand that until he told him what his wife had told him.

"You can set yourself up in a house right now and think that you'd never have to worry about money again. And even if you only paid your mortgage once a month, you'd be just fine with the interest you have coming in on your money. But is it enough interest? Do you have it set up so that the money goes back to the big pot, or do you have little pots that need to be fed? You know, like utilities. A car payment. Is the car going to last you as long as the truck did? That's a no if you're wondering. They don't make them like that anymore. But these little pots have to be fed or they'll die too. Figure out what kind of outgoing money you want and how to make that happen so that you have income, too. You don't have to get a job, but keeping your money is hard work, and you have to deal with it every day. Asking questions and doing something now before it's too late is the best way. But if you just get some answers and never do anything about them, then you've just wasted your money on something else. Understand?" He said that he did, for now. "Good. That means you'll have more questions. I should have thought about you guys and having money right now. I'll set the six of you up with some people that will help you grow what you have so that even twenty years from now, you'll still be considered wealthy men with smarts."

He'd thanked him a great deal about that. He was going to listen and take notes, too. Raphael said that he didn't want to make the same mistakes that he'd made, and Wylie thought that he was all right with that. He had made some mistakes, but he was well on his way to fixing them, too.

"You guys can stay with us until you get things squared away." He thought his brother was joking until he realized that Kinsey didn't joke when it came to things about life. "There is plenty of room. We're going to be having some work done on the house, but like I said, there is plenty of room for all of us."

"I might take you up on that. I hate the house that I'm in. I'm going to have someone come in and look over the structure of it and see if it can be fixed. Then I'm going to rent it out so that I can have it off my back for a while." He asked about condos. "I'm not sure about that just yet. I never would have thought of people being that close to us all the time, and us not being used to it. I think Raphael had it right in saying that we're like old men with no wives who are sort of set in our ways. We have to work up to having neighbors."

The next morning, a construction crew showed up by way of David, and he was told that the hallway wasn't going to structurally hurt them if they tore it out. he had them do that and to upgrade the kitchen. Kinsey had told him that an upgraded kitchen would bring in the bigger renters rather than ones who would bail on him in a few months. Not that higher renters meant that he'd get the cream of the crop, but he stood a better chance of getting someone who would appreciate the house more than most.

His first time with the attorney was in just over an hour, and he and Raphael decided they could get breakfast out and not disturb the construction crew that was already tearing out walls. He might take his brother up on his offer simply because he didn't think that he could handle all the mess that was going on. Besides, David would be close, and he could get things answered without hoping to run into the older man.

Bodi and Gleason met them at the little restaurant and had a meal with them, too. He realized that he didn't know where everyone was staying until then. Apparently, they were all renting rooms at the local B&B until they figured out what they were doing. Ara and Kinsey were going to meet them at the offices and get the training they all needed.

~*~

Meggie waited for her turn at the bank counter. She didn't have much to do today and was looking forward to it. She was going to go with a realtor to figure out some condos for the other men, and then she was free for the rest of the day. She hoped they'd stay with them while they were getting their feet wet, but she could also understand why they'd want their own space, too. They were going to live in a condo together until they each found a home. She didn't think that was going to work, but she had to give them credit for trying to make it work for them.

"Can I ask you about the Pennington brothers?" She said, sure but told her that she wasn't going to give her phone numbers. "That's all right. I just wanted to see if they have all that money from the sale of their farm? Do you know if they're looking for dates?"

"I think they're just getting used to having money right now." She didn't answer either question about the money or dates. That seemed too personal. "I'd like to put my future husband on my accounts."

"You have to do that with Mr. Howard. He does all that stuff." She got her accounts deposited and was stepping away when she grabbed her arm. "You didn't say if they were dating or not. Me and the girls always thought that they were good-looking, and now that they have money, it makes them all the more appealing. If you know what I mean."

"I believe that I do." Glancing at the name tag that was on her blouse, she made a mental note to talk to Mr. Howard about her. She had a feeling that Candance would cause trouble if the men were ever to open an account in the local bank. Not that she'd steal from them, but she wouldn't put it past her to blab around how much was in their accounts if someone were to ask. Or even not to ask.

Getting Kinsey put onto her accounts was a lot easier than she thought it would be. After telling him that he'd have to come into the bank sometime and sign off on the cards that would be required of him, she was ready to go. But she did stop long enough to talk to Mr. Howard about Candance and her inquiries about the Pennington family.

On her way home, she made a note to talk to the men about women and their ways. They weren't stupid, never that, but all they needed was for some woman to latch onto them who needed their family boosted up with some extra cash, and that would be terrible for them. She would talk to Kinsey first and ask him about it. Perhaps they knew what sort of women she was talking about and already knew what to look out for.

After getting her things put away, she checked on the destruction of the kitchen. It was going to be a mess for a lot longer than it would start to look like a kitchen again. Alice said that she'd not realized how outdated the room was until she was talking about a new refrigerator. They even had an intercom system in the room for phone calls that were routed through the room for the family.

Kinsey was out with his brothers today at an attorney's office. They were learning all kinds of things that someone with money all their life would have known. She was just going to sit in the library when the front doorbell rang. Going to the door, she was surprised to see Rosie there.

"Nothing is wrong." She said she had to say that when she was making a call at someone's house. "I usually say that when I'm also out making calls about teenagers. You know, no one is dead kind of thing."

"Come on in." Rosie said she felt stupid now for coming to talk to her. "It's all right, Rosie. I've known you since first grade, you can come to me anytime."

"Is Wylie dating anyone?" She had blurted it out so quickly that she noticed her face turn red. "I've had this major crush on him since he was a senior and I was a sophomore. And I knew you'd be honest with me about what you think about me asking him out. I'm not doing this because he's suddenly rich, but he might be dating more now that he doesn't have the farm taking up all his time. My friend used to date him—I was so jealous of her, but I found out that he'd been canceling on her all the time because he had to work. I like a man who knows his priorities when it comes to family and work." She laughed. "I'm making a mess of this, and I'm sorry to have bothered you."

"I don't know whether he's dating or not. They're pretty private about that." She invited Rosie in for some tea, and she told her that she was on her lunch break only. "I can ask him, but I think that it would be better if you were to ask him out. I know that he's getting used to things, and it might be good for him to have a normal date."

"Candance lost her job today." Well, that was good news. "I had to escort her home because she was too upset to drive. She mentioned that all she wanted to do was get some big money from the Penningtons. She didn't care which one. Startled me a bit if you want to know the truth. I hadn't thought of them having the money so much as the time it would be freeing up for them."

"She said the same thing to me." Rosie assured her that Candance didn't know who had told on her. She'd apparently been talking about them all day to anyone who was at her window." Shaking her head, she laughed a little. "Ballsy if you ask me. Trying to get a man to take her out so that she could hit him up for a loan to buy herself a house for them together."

"I didn't know she had been planning that far." Rosie said she had to run. "Ask him out, Rosie. Just like you did when you got here. Tell him about the crush and how you've been waiting for him to have some free time, too."

"I believe I will." She was gone in another few minutes, and Meggie had to laugh. Candance had been fired for wanting to make a play for one of the men, and she'd been in there to add one to her accounts. She wondered what she'd say about that.

She spent the rest of the day figuring out paint colors for the bedrooms. When five o'clock rolled around and she'd not heard from Kinsey, she decided to have herself something to tide her over as she'd skipped lunch. Just as she was putting away the peanut butter after making herself a peanut butter and jelly sandwich, the front door opened, and she could hear the men talking.

"They're going to stay here." She was delighted to hear that and told Kinsey that. Then she told them all about Candance and how she'd been wanting to get her hands on someone's money. "We've had some trouble with her before. Each one of us who had come home on leave would have her trying to 'date' one of us. It wasn't a date so much as us spending the night with her so that we could have a night full of fun. She also planned to get pregnant by one of us so she'd be set up for life as a war widow. Never could understand where the war widow part came from, but that's what she was telling everyone. She would blab around town how she was out to get her a service man and we were going to be her money bags."

"You'll have to be more careful of people wanting to 'date' the five of you, too. They might have more in mind than a night full of sex and drinking." All six of them told her that their grandma had told them about the women who only wanted one thing and how they should be careful. "Good. I don't want to have to bar any of you from our house when you find Miss Money Bags."

Each of them had an overnight bag and were going to work from that. They really didn't have much in the way of clothing, and she was hoping that they would have taken care of that. It seemed to her they were still having problems spending money on the necessities by not buying two different colored socks. She was still laughing when they all sat down to dinner about Raphael and his suit with socks.

They seemed to be happy with the way things went today, and that's what they talked about during dinner. About how much they'd learned in one sitting with the attorney, and were looking forward to tomorrow, too. She was glad they were getting help. She loved these men so much.

After dinner, she could tell that they were less stressed, and being under one roof helped. They were determined to make the money work for them rather than the other way around. Meggie was happy about that, they seemed to have a better handle on living arrangements, too. They wouldn't stay forever, but they would stay until they were ready to embark on their next adventure.

"Did you have any trouble at the bank other

than Candance?" She asked him what he meant. "I don't know. Did anyone tell you not to put me on your accounts? I don't know that they'd come right out and say that to you, but I don't know."

"No one would say that. And if they did, I'd get them fired, too. What a thing to think. Your credit cards will be here in the morning, so don't forget to check the mailbox." He said he'd get it when he went to class. "Are you having fun with the classes? Learning anything important?"

"So far, he's only been telling us about contracts. And what to look for in them. I very much enjoyed those, and I think my brothers did as well. Basically, he said that we'd need to find each of us an attorney so that we can send anything that needs our signature on it to them. He's going to give us a list of people that he trusts." She said that they had a family attorney and one for the business. "He told me that. He said that I could use yours for as much as you trust them, too."

They were headed to bed when she saw the men standing in the hallway. Asking them if everything was all right, they told her that they were just getting ready to go to bed and thought of telling her and Kinsey once again how much they appreciated what they were doing for them. And how they liked that they were able to stay somewhere like this house and be out of town.

"You having trouble with people in town?" It was Wylie who said that they needed a new school. And a larger grocery store. "I see. Hitting you up for funds now. If you keep telling them no, then they'll get the hint. But remember, never tell them that you're thinking about it. That will get you in more hot water."

"Jason, the attorney we were working with today said we should tell them that we were looking into our options, and we'll get back with them. Like you said, the town will benefit from the sale of the farm, and someday, when things start rolling with David, they'll see that." She told them that she was proud of them. "Good. Just so you know, we're glad to have you as being a part of the family. You've made Kinsey very happy, and that's all we ever wanted. To be happy."

"He makes me feel the same way. Happy and in love." She kissed each of them on the cheek and told them that she was here for them. When they went to the rooms they'd picked out, she made her way down the hall towards their room. Kinsey was already in bed but not asleep. She was glad; she had plans for him and his body.

"I have two questions for you." She told him to ask away. "When will you know if you're pregnant or not, and when you do, can we go get married at the courthouse, then later for a big wedding? David and Alice have their hearts set on a giant wedding. They want to use their new house for the reception." She laughed and said she could work with that. "Good. And so you know, I don't want to tell anyone about the baby for a while so that we can hold that secret close to us. All right?"

"Perfect." She got into bed with him after telling him what his brothers had said. "I think that they're going to do just fine, the five of them. Now, if they can find someone to love, then that would make their lives as perfect as ours is."

Before You Go...

HELP AN AUTHOR

write a review

THANK YOU!

Share your voice and help guide other readers to these wonderful books. Even if it's only a line or two your reviews help readers discover the author's books so they can continue creating stories that you'll love. Login to your favorite retailer and leave a review. Thank you.

Kathi S. Barton is an award-winning and bestselling author known for her steamy paranormal romances and unforgettable characters. A recipient of the prestigious Pinnacle Book Achievement Award, her books have topped the charts on Amazon and All Romance eBooks, earning her a loyal global readership.

Kathi lives in Nashport, Ohio, with her husband, Paul. When she's not crafting passionate love stories set in magical worlds, she enjoys camping, exploring local auctions, and attending county fairs, where Paul showcases his artwork and pottery. Her creative spark—fueled by a muse she describes as a cross between Jimmy Stewart and Hugh Jackman—brings her stories to vivid, heartfelt life.

Paranormal romance with plenty of heat is her favorite genre, and she loves connecting with her readers. Feel free to reach out—Kathi would love to hear from you.

Email: aaronskiss@gmail.com

Blog: kathisbartonauthor.blogspot.com